Prickly

Isl

&

the Emerald

Treasure

Christopher

Davies

ISBN:13:978-1511776639
ISBN-10:1511776633

Barny
Watch out for
the pirates!!
Christopher Davies

For Grandma Betty and Grandad Geoff who are very special to me and our family. Grandma has always had a fascination and love of nature and she also makes delicious flapjack which she calls 'crunch'!

Thank you

I would like to thank a few special people who helped me with this book.

Firstly, Mark for his innovative map and boat design and constant support with the story through to publication. Mum, for some lovely drawings and artistic support. Megan, for her creative ideas with the images and cover design. Laila, Erin, Reuben and Cam for very helpful feedback during the editing process.

I would also like to say a big thank you to Merryn, for her thoughtful and meticulous editing skills and her patience!

I would like to reserve a special thank you to Pixabay, for allowing me to use several of their drawings and images in this story.

Finally, I would like to say a massive thank you to you, the reader, for choosing this book. I hope you enjoy it.

Some of the names and locations in this book are factual but all of the characters and events are fictitious.

Chapter 1

The Quiz Show

Hi, my name is Jay and I would like to share something amazing with you.

About a year ago now, I left a chest full of treasure worth thousands of pounds on a desert island. It's true, I'm not lying – diamonds, emeralds, rubies – the lot!

You are probably thinking I was completely crazy or just plain stupid, but I wonder, would you have done the same in my situation?

It all started the day Dad was on TV in one of those peculiar quiz shows. He had to guess how many islands were in the Pacific Ocean (to the nearest thousand) and somehow he managed to get it right! Apparently there are 26,459 islands in total!

The quiz show was called, 'Did you Know?' but what I couldn't understand was how did THEY know? Had someone counted the islands one by one? It must have taken them a long time... months and months. I would have liked that job, sailing around the ocean for weeks on end. It sounded a lot more fun than school!

Mind you, they would never have asked me to do it. I find it difficult enough to add seventeen and ninety together, let alone hundreds and thousands. My mind just goes blank when I see numbers. In fact, it goes blank when I step inside school.

Dad's mind never goes blank though, even when you ask him difficult questions like the one on the quiz, he always comes up with the right answer. (But this time I think it might have been just a lucky guess.)

That night he won the Star Prize. A year in the South Pacific, on an island in French Polynesia – a desert island!

When I heard the quiz master announce the prize, I was so surprised, the stripes almost jumped off my football shirt!

A desert island! Where there might be buried treasure, blood-thirsty pirates, deadly killer sharks and best of all... NO SCHOOL!

I couldn't believe it. Nothing that good could happen to me – could it?

"Wait and see," said Mum, who looked more scared than excited, "Dad will be home later."

"Yes wait and see," echoed Sanjana my twin sister, who always repeated everything Mum and Dad said. It was a bit like having three parents in the house.

When Dad eventually arrived home in a pair of Hawaiian shorts and a plastic parrot stuck to his shoulder, I started to believe it actually WAS true! Then when Dad showed us a picture of the island and the four plane tickets which would take us most of the way, I knew it was no joke. We were going – for real!

Chapter 2

The Best Day Ever (almost)

The next few weeks flew by. Mum left her job, Dad left his job and then came the most exciting day of my life – the day I left school! I knew I would have to go back some day, but twelve months seemed like forever. A whole year free from dull, dreary lessons, mind-numbing maths and horrifying spelling tests!

At home-time, I tidied my desk for the last time and said goodbye to my friends. I was going to miss them.

"Any room in your suitcase for me?" joked Max, who always played football with me.

"Sorry, no space left," I replied, cheerfully. "But I wish you could come with us. All of you!"

"If you're taking anyone, it will be me!" joked Mrs May, my favourite teaching assistant, who always helped me loads with my work.

"Have a fantastic time and be careful," said Mrs May, pointing to where we were going on the world map. "What an incredible experience you are going to have!"

Then something happened that really spoilt the day. Just as Mum arrived to collect us, Sanjana started to cry.

"What's the matter, dear?" asked Mrs Jones, my class teacher, kindly.

"They're all going to be better than me when I get back!" she blubbered. "I'll probably have to go back and do the same year again!"

When Sanjana cries the whole world gets to hear about it and Mum came to the rescue as usual. What's more she promised Sanjana that she wouldn't get behind in her work because she would be teaching BOTH of us every single day of our holiday!

It was at this moment that I realised the big disadvantage of having a teacher for a parent, not to mention a 'swotty' Sanjana for a twin sister...

I was MAD!

* * *

Chapter 3

A Flapjack Farewell

I didn't stay mad for long though, I was too excited about our adventure. We had travelled to India before in the summer holidays, to see Mum's family in Delhi, but this was going to be different. This was a small island on the other side of the world!

We finished off our last minute packing and then we all went round to Grandma's house for tea.

As soon as we arrived, Grandad gave me an old telescope that he had used in the war. It was made of brass and although it looked small, Grandad showed me how it pulled out to about a half a metre long! It also had a cork cover and strap so you could hang it round you neck.

"Keep it with you at all times, young Jay. It could be very useful on a desert island."

"Thanks, Grandad! I will," I replied, trying it out across the dining room. "It's brilliant! I can see Grandma's chocolate cake and it looks enormous!"

"I wish I was coming with you, Jay!" continued Grandad, excitedly. "What a fantastic adventure it's going to be. If only I was 10 years younger..."

Grandma had made the biggest tea ever! A fantastic spread of sandwiches, cheese and chive crisps, hot sausage rolls, big chunky chips, fresh fruit salad and the yummiest chocolate cake in the world!

"Keep eating everyone," cried Grandma insistently. "You won't be getting another decent meal for a long time!"

"But I'm full, Grandma, honest."

"Nonsense, Jay!", she smiled, sneaking more chocolate cake onto my plate. "Got to build your strength up. You're going to be out in the wild with bloodthirsty pirates in a few days! Not to mention the sharks!"

We all laughed and continued eating and joking for a while.

(Little did we know that Grandma might be right...)

We were all having a lovely time, but then I started feeling a bit nervous. Tomorrow we were going and life would never be the same...

"Be ever so careful!" warned Grandma, getting a bit tearful and giving us all hugs and kisses goodbye. "Remember to phone or text."

"There won't be any signal out there, Grandma," sighed Sanjana, sadly.

"Sorry!"

"Maybe a message in a bottle then?" joked Grandma. "Don't forget us!"

"Of course we won't Grandma," I replied, giving her a huge hug. "That could never happen!"

"We will send you some postcards if we can!" cried Sanjana, enthusiastically.

"It won't all be plain sailing," said Grandad, suddenly looking more serious. "There will be difficult days ahead. Look after each other and remember to respect the island and its people."

"We are the only people!" exclaimed Dad. "It's just the four of us and the parrots."

"Well respect the island and the parrots, son," replied Grandad. "It's their home. You are only visiting the island for a year remember!"

Mum gave Grandma instructions about feeding Millie (our cat) and then it was time to go.

Grandma was looking upset again so I gave her the biggest hug ever. I was feeling upset too.

Then Grandma gave me a big container full of my favourite flapjack!

"Share it with your sister, you hear! Goodbye!"

* * *

Chapter 4

The Journey

We flew out from Heathrow airport at 19:45 on flight 342. At last the waiting was over, we were off to the South Pacific! We were all extremely excited – even Mum and Dad!

We stopped at Los Angeles for re-fueling and then flew on to the island of Tahiti. It was the middle of the night still so we couldn't see much. After an hour or two waiting in the airport lounge we got onto a small plane which took us to another island in the region. During the flight Sanjana started to chatter about things she had read about it.

"This island is famous!" she announced, sounding like a newsreader from the BBC. "Film stars come here for their holidays... I wonder if we will see any?"

As we were coming in to land the Captain's voice came over the intercom.

"Welcome to Bora Bora everybody! This is a very special island and is known by locals as the island to make your dreams a reality. Enjoy your stay!"

"What does reality mean, Dad?" I asked.

"It means for real. Make your dreams real." replied Dad, still half engrossed in his 'Build-it' magazine.

"Make your dreams come true!" replied Mum, excitedly.

"I can see why they say that." I said quietly to myself, as I glanced through the window.

It was starting to get light. I couldn't see any film stars, but I could see why they wanted to come here. The scenery was amazing! There was lush green everywhere, golden beaches of sand and a cluster of peaks that looked like volcanoes. It was breathtaking!

Chapter 5

Sacred Radimatu

We landed safely and had a quick breakfast in the airport café.

"Eat it up!" nagged Mum. "It's mati, their local fruit, it won't hurt you!"

I managed to eat most of the red berries and it actually tasted quite nice.

Then it was on to the next part of our journey. We went down to the harbour and met up with a man called Takootu. He was a local man who had been asked by the TV channel in England to take us to our island. He looked about the same age as Grandad, but he was taller and looked much stronger. He had jet black hair and his dark skin was covered in unusual tattoos.

"Hello, family Smith!" he said smiling cheerfully and shaking all our hands energetically. "Me is your guide and I am taking you to your island."

His English wasn't perfect but we could understand what he was saying and none of us spoke the local language of Tahitian.

Takootu led us towards an old wooden sailing boat which looked rather sad and unstable. The painted hull had peeled away in patches and the sail looked tattered and torn. It had seen better days.

"This is 'Captain Cook'," he announced proudly. "We sail in it now. Please you get in family Smith."

Mum looked alarmed and started moaning to Dad that the boat looked almost as old as the real Captain Cook – a famous explorer who discovered Bora Bora in 1769! Takootu seemed to understand that Mum was a little anxious about the boat and smiled reassuringly.

"Boat old but strong!" Takootu added, as he loaded on the last of our luggage.

Within minutes we were in the open water. Sea birds glided above us and blue dolphins swam close by, as though they were trying to talk to us.

The sun shone brightly and away in the distance we could see many tiny islands dotted all around. One of these islands was going to be our new home! I got out Grandad's telescope and gazed through it admiring the wonderful view.

Takootu was a good guide and had

lived in the area since he was a boy. He told us all about the islands we passed.

"Is that our island?" asked Sanjana, looking towards a large green island to our right.

"No," replied Takootu steering the boat parallel to the shore. "This is Radimatu!"

"Radimatu!" exclaimed Sanjana excitedly. "That's in my book! Isn't it famous for something?"

"You is wise girl," smiled Takootu. "Yes, Tahitians believe it is the place of Zeo."

"Got it!" cried Sanjana, eagerly scrutinising her guide book of the islands. "Sacred Radimatu! Birth place of the Tahitian God Zeo!"

Sanjana was sounding more and more like Dad every day, she knew everything! Sanjana carried on reading more and more facts about it. I was just starting to get bored when she mentioned the word 'WAR'!

"War?" I cricd eagerly.

"Yes, Zeo is the God of war and new life," continued Sanjana. "Tahitians were very fierce warriors and fighters apparently."

"Still are!" shouted Dad, "Did you see them in the Rugby World Cup? They were brutal!"

"Is that true, Takootu?" I inquired.

"Yes, my young friend, long time ago, there is lots of fighting, always the fighting - every island doing it! Very sad."

The area looked so beautiful and peaceful now, it was hard to imagine it was once like a war zone.

"What were they fighting about?" I asked.

"Plenty things my young friend. They fight for the land, for food and the pearls of course."

"What real pearls? Like in the pirate films?" I asked, suddenly feeling very excited.

"Black pearls, emeralds and other jewels. They is always fighting over it. They steal it from Radimatu!"

"What, ACTUAL treasure!?" I cried excitedly, not believing it could be true.

"Yes, real treasure my friend."

Takootu went on to tell us how treasure of all description had been brought from far-off lands to the shores of Radimatu to honour the God Zeo.

"But not all the islands did believe in Zeo and some is greedy and one day the Bandi stole the treasure!"

"What like pirates?" Sanjana inquired

inquisitively.

"Yes, they is pirates," replied Takootu, his eyes full of sorrow. "They took it all - every single jewel - gone!"

"But what happened then? Didn't the Radimatu islanders fight them and try to get it back?" I shouted, beginning to feel that poor Takootu and his people had been wronged by these cowardly thieves!

"Yes, of course my friend. There was big, big troubles. The people of Radimatu went all crazy! Big search and big fights with the Bandi but no one is finding it. Hidden somewhere, lost forever..."

"The lost Treasure of Radimatu!" cried Sanjana triumphantly, peering into her guide book. "Stolen on the night of 29th May 1716 and never seen again..."

"That is it, my girl... a terrible night," replied Takootu looking even sadder than before.

"If someone did manage to find the treasure, their dreams really would come true!" said Dad excitedly, remembering what the flight Captain had said earlier. "Has anyone got any idea where it might be hidden?"

"No one is knowing, Mr Smith," continued Takootu gloomily. "Some say it lies at bottom of the ocean but I have the feeling, a feeling strong in my bones, that it is still with us. Buried on an island close by, but who knows which one...?"

We all gazed out to sea. All we could see was island upon island - hundreds of them! It would be like looking for a lost pebble on a stony beach.

Chapter 6

Gigantuki Island

In the next half hour we must have passed dozens of small islands. Any one of these islands could have been the home of the lost treasure. There were narrow ones, round ones, rocky ones and tree-covered ones. So many I lost count. I was still daydreaming about pirates and pearls when I suddenly heard Takootu shouting.

"There it is!" he yelled excitedly. "Gigantuki Island. Your island, family Smith!"

We all looked to where Tukootu was pointing and there before our eyes was the most beautiful sight we had ever seen! The entire island was covered in a lush green forest of tropical palm trees, that seemed to glimmer and shimmer in the bright sunlight like a priceless emerald. Below the canopy there were multi-coloured plants and flowers of all shapes and sizes.

As we sailed closer, we could make out a huge black rock (which looked like a small volcano) rising up from the centre, with a spectacular waterfall cascading down onto the sandy beach below. Small blue waves stroked the shore and as the water became shallower we could see brightly coloured fish zigzagging in the depths below. It looked so magical and it was going to be our home for a whole year!

"Look!" shouted Mum, eagerly. "I can see birds and parrots in the trees! Red ones and green!"

"I can see monkeys too!" I shouted enthusiastically, peering through grandad's telescope.

"I didn't think monkeys lived in these islands, Takootu?" questioned Dad, knowledgeably.

"It is true, Mr Smith!" replied Takootu, cheerfully. "Not many islands is having monkeys, but people who live here long before bring monkeys from South America, and now there is lots!"

Monkeys on our island! This was too good to be true! Maybe I could make a new friend?

We were almost ashore now. Takootu steered the 'Captain Cook' towards the huge waterfall, spray falling like a fine mist all around us, sparkling in the dazzling sunlight like glittering jewels.

"Water is deeper here," he explained cheerfully. "Safe for boat!"

Takootu carefully set the boat ashore and within a few moments we were all taking our first steps on Gigantuki Island! Takootu pointed at the water cascading down.

"Fresh water!" he cried, throwing the water over his face and allowing it to flow into his mouth. "Fresh spring. You drink!"

We were all very hot and thirsty after our long journey and glad to quench our thirst in the cool, crystal clear spring water. Within seconds, Takootu appeared with two large coconuts. He smashed them on the rock and broke them carefully into smaller pieces.

"You is hungry, family Smith?" he asked, handing us all a piece. We all nodded gratefully and tucked into our new island snack. The coconut tasted so sweet and yummy. Almost as good as Grandma's flapjack!

"You look after the island," smiled Takootu, "and the island is looking after you!"

It reminded me of what Grandad had said before we left.

"You in charge now family Smith. Everything you need is here."

As we ate and drank, we could hear exotic birds squawking and monkeys chattering, I couldn't wait to explore.

"Why is it called Gigantuki island?" asked Mum, as Takootu started to show us around.

"Because everything is being a bit bigger than normal – no one is knowing why," replied Takootu, pointing ahead. "The palm trees and the parrots, the flowers and the fruit. All is being bigger. Look!"

All around us we could see giant palm trees, giant parrots and giant pineapples! Everything WAS slightly bigger than normal. Takootu was right!

"I hope there aren't any giant sharks!" cried Sanjana, looking slightly concerned. "Or giant wasps!"

We all laughed and continued to explore. The canopy of the palm trees protected us from the strong sunlight and as we walked Takootu pointed to all the exotic fruits we could eat, and the one's we couldn't. There were giant lemons, limes, avocados, pineapples and water melons. We could have fresh fruit salad every day.

"Look out, everyone! A giant spider!" I cried.

Sanjana froze to the spot, shuddering with fear – she has always been petrified of spiders. Then suddenly she realised I was only joking.

"I'll get you, pest!" she cried, crossly, sprinting after me like a young Tahitian chief going into battle!

Luckily there is one thing I can do better than Sanjana – RUN! She can never catch me!

I waited for them further on and hid up a giant palm tree. When I jumped out and surprised them all, only Takootu seemed to find it funny. Dad just gave me a lecture on how I should be kinder to my sister and we continued exploring.

After a while, Takootu showed us a safe place to make camp. He said it would be shielded from the wind and rain by the volcano-shaped rock, and would also be close to the freshwater spring. Then Takootu showed us where the dead wood was for building.

"Takootu not cut down living tree to build shelter," he explained arriving at some trees closer to the beach. "I is using the dead wood."

Takootu started cutting the wood carefully and Sanjana and I were allowed to help.

"There is big storm last month. Many trees is being hit. Very good wood for tree-house!"

After cutting the wood to the right size, Takootu helped us build an amazing shelter. Not that Dad needed much help, as he loved making things himself. Within a couple of hours it was all done.

It was a kind of multi-layered tree-house spanning two giant palm trees. We had a downstairs area to eat and then there were three bedroom areas, and mine was the highest of them all – at the top! Dad and Takootu had used the dead wood to make a kind of floor and we had wooden walls in each area too, so we were protected from the wind and the SPIDERS! Well that's what Mum assured Sanjana!

* * *

Soon it was time for Takootu to leave.

"I is coming back next month, OK?" said Takootu, shaking our hands again. "Goodbye family Smith! And remember, look after the island and the island is looking after you!"

We all thanked Takootu and waved him off on the 'Captain Cook'.

We were all alone now on a desert island in the middle of the South Pacific Ocean. Our adventure had only just begun.

* * *

Chapter 7

Monkey Business!

Our first night in our tree-house was scary! There were very strange sounds coming from everywhere and none of us could sleep very well. We all ended up in Mum and Dad's room playing cards until late. Eventually we must have fallen asleep.

The next morning we were all a bit tired and grumpy but Mum still made us do our school work and that made me even grumpier.

'Lessons in the morning – free time in the afternoon.'

"Yes!" cried Sanjana eagerly, "I'll get the books!"

"But Mum, it's our first day on the island! I don't want to do maths and spelling – I want to explore!"

"No moaning Jay, unless you want lessons ALL day!" replied Mum in her strict classroom voice. "Best to get into good habits straight away."

I wasn't happy but Mum did make the lessons quite enjoyable that morning and there was no maths or spelling! To start, we made our first entry in our diary and I wrote all about our journey and Takootu. For art, we went down to the beach and made sketches of the rock pools. Then for PE, we had races on the sand and then went for a swim in the shallow lagoon.

"This is much better than school!" I cried, floating on my back in the clear, warm water.

"See," said Mum, cheerfully. "Learning can be fun!"

"Can we do maths and spelling

tomorrow?" moaned Sanjana.

After lunch I spent the whole afternoon exploring, in fact I did that every afternoon for the first week. The island was truly amazing! There was so much to see and do. There were sandy beaches to play on, rock pools to fish in, giant palm trees to climb up and best of all, giant water falls to slide down. It was better than any holiday camp I knew!

The only problem was that I had no one to share all the fun with. Dad was always busy making something, Mum was always busy drawing or painting exotic plants or birds and as for Sanjana; you can probably guess what she was always doing? That's right, her schoolwork!

As I sat eating some sweet pink fruit under the cool canopy of the palm trees, I started to feel a tiny bit lonely. If only I had one of my school friends with me, I thought. There was so much we could be doing...

All of a sudden, a small coconut crashed on the ground next to me! I looked to where I thought it had come from and there, perched high in a palm tree, was a cheeky white-faced monkey!

It was staring straight at me and then it started to make a loud chattering sound. It seemed excited. Then all of a sudden another coconut came flying out of the tree and narrowly missed my nose!

I looked up again and saw a pink-faced monkey swinging around and around on its branch and chattering excitedly. Was this some sort of game they were playing? Maybe I should throw one back? Then all of a sudden, I saw another GIANT coconut hurtling towards me and another and another! I was under attack!

Before I had time to take cover one of the giant coconuts hit me smack on the head! I fell to the ground, dazed and lay still.

I'm not exactly sure what happened next but I remember opening my eyes and the first thing I saw sitting next to me, was a cheeky white-faced monkey. The monkey from the tree! It had orangey brown fur and stood about half a metre tall. It had a very long tail and a very cute, cheeky white face. He wasn't chattering like before, if anything he looked almost sad.

My head was pounding and I could feel a huge bump coming up just above my right ear. Suddenly, the monkey held up a yellow plant and started rubbing it on his head energetically. Then he held out the yellow plant to me and jumped up and down chattering. I wasn't sure but I got the feeling that he wanted me to take the plant and rub it on my head. Like rubbing dock leaves on your arm after a nettle sting, I suppose.

So that's just what I did! I rubbed the yellow plant onto my head and within minutes the swelling had gone down and the pounding had subsided. It was like magic!

From that day on, my life on the island became much more fun! I now had a new friend and I named him Minoo.

We played together all the time. Hide-and-seek, tig and coconut catch. One afternoon I taught Minoo how to play football, with a hollowed-out coconut. It was going really well until Minoo tried to score with a header. He ended up with a bump on his head almost as big as the giant coconut! We needed the special yellow plant again but this time it was for him!

"I told you not to head it!" I cried sympathetically to Minoo, as I rubbed in the leaves.

The next day, Minoo taught me how to do some of his monkey tricks high up in the trees with his friends.

It was a bit scary at first, but I soon got the hang of it. Well, I thought I had. I was hanging upside down from a branch, just like Minoo, making chattering noises with his monkey friends and feeling quite proud of myself, when suddenly I heard a creaking sound... it was my branch!

The next moment I heard a loud
CRACK!!

Seconds later I was tumbling towards the ground, at what seemed like a zillion miles an hour...

* * *

Chapter 8

Prickly-Pong!

I landed with a huge CRASH in the undergrowth! The spot couldn't have been worse. It was covered by a mass of small spiky plants, whose leaves and stems were as prickly as a hedgehog!

Minoo found my spectacular fall extremely amusing and was laughing so much he almost fell out of the tree himself. But I was in no mood to joke, as a large mass of the spiky spines were now sticking right into my back. What's more, there was still a far worse pain to come...

"Ouch!!" I yelled, as Minoo pulled out the first prickly spine. "No!!" I groaned, as he took out another.

Minoo ignored my cries and continued to pull the rest of them out one by one.

"Ouch!! Ouch!! OUCH!!!!"

When Minoo finally removed the last prickly spine, it felt as though my whole back had caught fire. I was about to cool it down in the sea when I noticed a strange purple substance all over my arms. It was coming from the big red flowers of the prickly plant – they were actually squirting at me!

The purple gunge was all sticky and

slimy. It looked and felt repulsive but it smelt even worse. In fact, it was the worst smell I had ever smelt in my life! Worse than the stinkiest stink bomb, worse than Jamie Roberts' smelly trainers and even worse than the sickening stench of sprouts for school dinners. It was revolting!

Minoo wiped the purple gunge off my arms with the leaf of a palm tree and gave me some coconut juice to rub all over, which made me smell a lot better. Then he squeezed some juice from a pink furry fruit to rub into my wounds and like magic the pain vanished, almost immediately!

Minoo was not only a good friend he was turning out to be an amazing doctor too. How did he know that certain plants had special healing powers? It was incredible. He was so clever!

I decided to call the spiky red plant, 'Prickly-Pong' (for obvious reasons) and ran back to camp to tell the others. As I ran, I noticed that there was Prickly-Pong under all the palm trees - it was everywhere!

"If there was any giant Prickly-Pong we really would be in trouble!" I joked to the others, as I told them about my fall and new discovery.

"You poor thing," said Mum, sympathetically, looking at my 'war-wounds'. "That sounded a nasty slip!" Mum suddenly pulled away and made a face and I could tell she must have caught a whiff of the smelly purple gunge.

"Trust you to go and discover something smelly and horrible!" sighed Dad. "Why couldn't you find something nice like your sister?"

"I did! I did!" I protested, excitedly. I started to tell them about the pink furry fruit Minoo had given me and how it was like a magic medicine, but they didn't seem that interested. Then Sanjana appeared with a folder with some amazing drawings of butterflies she had sketched on the island. They were all sorts of colours and she had named each one herself.

"What do you think?" Sanjana asked eagerly.

"They're not bad," I said, reluctantly, feeling a bit jealous. "I like the one with the blue wings best."

Not only was Sanjana a good reader, she was also a great drawer, just like mum. During supper I sat there trying to think of something I could do that would be special. Something unique, better than 'super-smart' Sanjana for a change. Then just as I was gulping down my third shell of coconut milk I had an idea. I would make a MAP of the island. That would do it!

Chapter 9

The Map

After morning lessons the next day, I got started on the map right away. Minoo knew the island like the back of his little hand, so he could help me.

Our first stop was Giant Rock. We climbed right to the top and from there we could see the outline pattern of the entire island. It was shaped like a figure of eight, with Giant Rock right in the centre. I drew the coast line carefully onto a large piece of paper Mum had given me from the school box. Next, I marked on Giant Rock and the waterfall, I called it 'Takootu Falls' as it reminded me of when we first arrived. I was missing Takootu, I wondered what he was up to and when he would visit us again.

Then I thought up a few more names to go along the coast, 'Dolphin Bay', 'Turtle Cove' and 'Shark Sands' where I had seen a shark! (but nobody else believed me).

After a while, we climbed down from Giant Rock and set off to explore. Minoo was an excellent guide, he knew every single square metre of the island. It was just as well I had my trainers on, because there was Prickly-Pong everywhere and those thorns were sharp!

As we went along, I marked down all the important things on my map. The beaches, the caves and the woods where Minoo and all his monkey friends lived, which I named 'Monkey-Mad-House'. I also marked on the spring and named it Zeo's Oasis, as Takootu had told us Zeo was the God of new life (as well as war). Minoo was looking a little left out, so I named the boggy area near the spring 'Minoo's

Marsh' and that soon cheered him up!

I also made up some silly names for places, like I'd seen on maps in books. Parrot Paradise, Coconut Copse and Jay's Jump, where I had fallen out of my tree! But my favourite name was Giant Spider Spot, which I put in especially for you-know-who!

Once I had finished all the names, I coloured the coast and waterfall blue, the cave black and the rest light green. Then I drew loads of tiny red circles all over the place to represent the 'Prickly-Pong'. Next I drew a compass at the top right hand corner and marked on north, south, east and west. Finally, I wrote 'Gigantuki Island' in bold at the top and put a huge cross where our tree-house was. There, it was finished!

"What do you think?" I asked, holding it up to Minoo, feeling quite proud of myself. Minoo jumped up and down chattering. I think that meant he liked it.

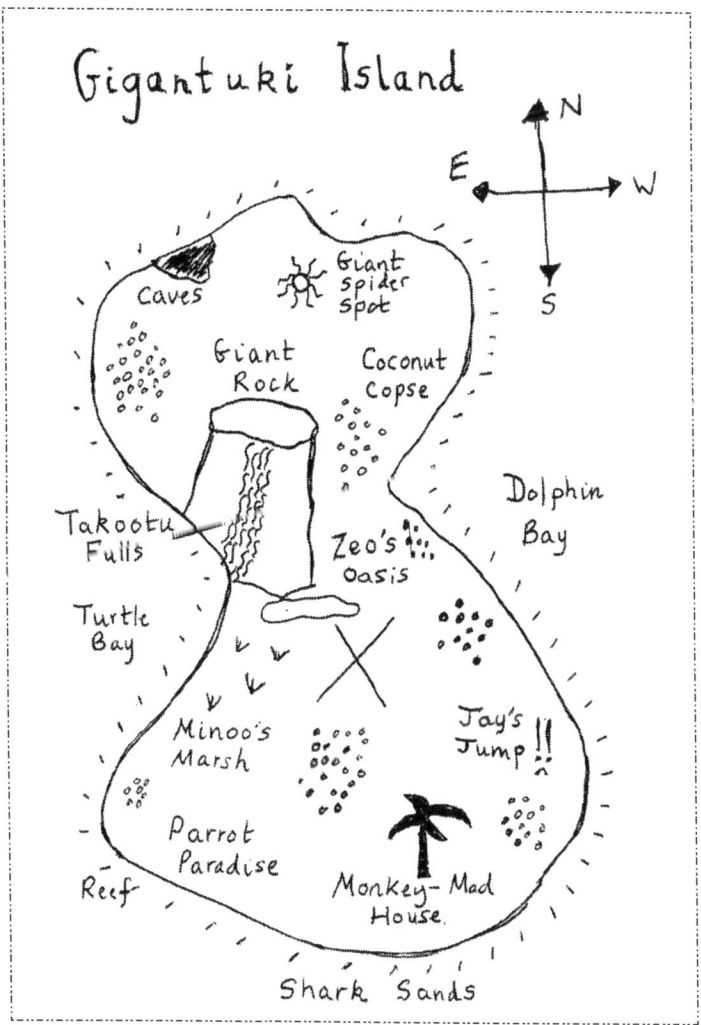

I ran back to camp excitedly to show the others but Dad wasn't so impressed.

"Look!" he sighed. "You've got your 'east' and 'west' mixed up. Don't they teach you the points of the compass at school anymore?"

"Yes we did that last term, remember Jay?" smirked Sanjana.

"Well I think it's wonderful!" said Mum cheerfully. "It's got so much detail and I love all the names of the places."

"Yes but a map is supposed to help you find things, not get you completely lost!" joked Dad. "Take a look at your sister's – she's got it right."

I couldn't believe it, Sanjana proceeded to roll out her own map of the island! Sure enough the compass points were in the right place and everything else looked in place too. It was immaculate.

"Dad said it's as good as the one's in

the University bookstore!" boasted Sanjana smugly.

I was stunned and angry. All my positive feelings about my map suddenly disappeared. There was no doubt Sanjana's map was really good but I wasn't going to let her know it. I felt like ripping it into pieces! She had stolen my idea and worse still, she had done it even better.

"Copy-cat!" I shouted angrily.

I knew Sanjana hated that word. It was the biggest insult to her because she prided herself on being the first and best at everything.

"Quiet!" ordered Dad, firmly.

"It was my idea first, you just copied me!" I cried. "Copy-cat! Copy-cat!" I chanted loudly in her face.

Sanjana protested for a while and then burst into tears.

"I did not! You're just jealous!"

"Enough!" bellowed Dad loudly, springing to his feet. "That's the end of it!"

When Dad said that was the end of it you knew it was. I was told to say sorry to Sanjana but I refused and so I was sent to my tree cabin with no supper.

* * *

I sat in my room in silence, feeling really upset. I felt angry and sorry all at the same time. I could hear the others eating and laughing below. Time seemed to pass by really slowly.

Then suddenly I heard Minoo chattering outside in the trees. I looked out and there he was, perched on the cabin roof, holding a vine in his hand! The vine was like a big green rope, so I grabbed hold of it too and we swung swiftly down to the ground – narrowly missing another patch of Prickly-Pong! I had escaped!

I spent the next hour on Giant Rock gazing out to sea. Minoo wanted to play coconut-catch but I wasn't in the mood. All I could think about was my map. I still liked it, even if no one else did.

After a while I decided to launch it in a bottle that I had found. Maybe someone else would find it miles and miles away and really like it? Maybe, just maybe, Grandma would find it? In any case, it would have an exciting adventure!

I unscrewed the top, pushed my map carefully into the bottle and then screwed the top back on tightly. Then I threw the bottle into the ocean with all my might! It was a good throw. I saw it land beyond the reef with a small splash.

It bobbed up and down for a while and then it started moving away on the current. It got smaller and smaller until it was a just a dot on the horizon.

It might float all the way to America or even England, I thought, you never know...

* * *

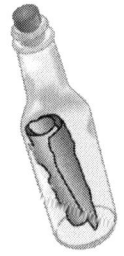

Chapter 10

The Trick

The next morning I woke up early and decided to play a trick on everyone. They would see the funny side, wouldn't they?

I laid the table for breakfast, really quietly, and left a note saying I had gone fishing with Minoo. Then I did a rather naughty thing! (I think I was still a bit mad from the night before).

I put Prickly-Pong on Sanjana's breakfast seat and I put some gunge from the flowers into Dad's coconut milk. It turned the milk light purple, but I was sure Dad wouldn't notice - he'd still be half asleep. Minoo helped me, and when we had finished we climbed up a big coconut tree close by. From here we had a brilliant view, as we didn't want to miss any of the fun!

We weren't disappointed either. As soon as Sanjana sat down on the Prickly-Pong, she shot up into the air like a rocket going into orbit! At the same time Dad took a huge gulp of his milk and almost immediately spat it out all over the table! Mum wasn't at all impressed. She started screaming and shouting. Then she told them that the pigs on her Uncle's farm back in India had better table manners than the pair of them!

Minoo and I found the whole scene hysterical and were laughing so much we almost fell out of the tree. But when Dad found the Prickly-Pong on Sanjana's seat and I heard him shout, "I'll murder him!" - I thought it was definitely time to be going.

We hid up at Giant Rock. Dad could never be bothered to climb up that high. When we reached the top, it was by far the best view on the island - you could see for miles. I was just gazing out to sea and wondering about my bottle and how far it might have gone, when I suddenly noticed something on the horizon. I pulled out my telescope to get a clearer view and peered through it excitedly.

I could see it now – it was a ship! A ship and it was heading straight for our island! Maybe, it was Takootu, I thought? It would be lovely to see him again...

As the ship got closer and closer, I could see a flag on the top of the mast. I focused on the flag and paused in disbelief. I couldn't believe my eyes...

* * *

Chapter 11

Pirates!

The flag was black with a white skull and crossbones in the centre – just like in all the films. Yes, the PIRATE films! It was a pirate ship! And what's more it was full of fierce, mean-looking men who looked very much like PIRATES!

I ran back to camp as fast as I could and told the others, but Dad thought it was some sort of game.

"Pirates?" he scoffed angrily, looking like he was going to feed me to the sharks. "Don't you think you've played enough silly jokes today already?"

I tried to explain but he wouldn't listen, none of them would. They were still mad about the trick I had played on them earlier that morning. Then suddenly we heard voices close by coming from the beach.

"What's that?" said Dad, starting to look alarmed. "It must be Takootu and his friends."

"Takootu isn't due to come this week, Dad," chipped in Sanjana, also beginning to look slightly worried.

"Well then who on earth is it...?" replied Dad, as the strange voices got louder and louder.

"It's the PIRATES!" I whispered insistently.

"Pirates indeed! What utter nonsense!" cried Dad, beginning to look annoyed again.

"If you don't believe me, take a look!"

Dad grabbed the telescope off me and gazed towards the beach. Suddenly he froze and turned a pale grey colour.

"They do look like p..p..PIRATES!" he stammered, anxiously.

Mum instantly turned white with fright and so did Sanjana.

"Quick!" I whispered, urgently. "We need to hide all our stuff and then get out of here!"

We spent the next couple of minutes frantically hiding everything away in the tree house. We just hoped they wouldn't notice anything...

"Follow him! They'll be here any second!" I cried, peering through my telescope.

Minoo was making his way up a huge palm tree about thirty metres away from our tree-house. He sat on the first branch, gesturing to us to follow him. Trees were useful things, I thought.

"I can't climb up there!" cried Sanjana

getting into a panic. "You know I'm scared of heights!"

"Which are you scared of more?" I pleaded. "Heights or PIRATES?"

Sanjana paused for a moment but when she heard the strange voices getting louder and louder, she shot up the tree almost as fast as Minoo.

Before long, we were all high up in the canopy safely out of view, we hoped. My heart was pounding and I had a terrible sick feeling in my stomach. Now all we had to do was be quiet. Very, very quiet...

A few moments later the pirates were

beneath us. There must have been about thirty of them! They were all dressed much like the pirates I had seen in the old films, not like the modern pirates I had seen on the news.

It was difficult to see much detail between the leaves and the coconuts, but with my telescope I could get glimpses of them every now and then. A few were carrying swords or shovels and nearly all of them had shiny daggers tucked into their belts. Some had long beards, others had short beards but they all looked menacing and mean.

Then I noticed one of them who looked meaner and more menacing than all the others put together! He was a huge man of about forty, with wild dark hair, a dense black beard and a patch over his left eye. His face looked wind-battered and worn, as if he had spent countless years at sea.

He looked very different to the others.

He was dressed quite smartly, like a gentlemen from long ago. He was wearing a thick black jacket, a stylish red belt and a triangular black hat edged with gold. In his right hand, he was holding a long silver sword, and he seemed like a man that wasn't afraid to use it!

"This be the spot!" announced the meanest looking one, studying the map in his left hand.

"Shall we start digging, Captain Red?" asked a tall, thin pirate with a long black moustache.

"Of course we shall, first mate Drummond!" replied the Captain sharply, in a strong west-country accent. "We didn't come to this dull little island to sunbathe! We can do that back at Weston-Super-Mare when we get home!"

Some of the pirates started to laugh at this last remark.

"I don't know what you are finding so funny!" snarled the Captain, turning to face them. "There is treasure in this ground before us, that once belonged to my family three hundred years since and I don't want to be waiting no longer to get my hands on it. So get you a digging! You lazy land-lubbers!"

"Aye! Aye! Captain!" replied the pirates dutifully and within minutes they were all hard at work - well most of them were.

There was a small group just below us and they seemed to be playing cards. Captain Red hadn't noticed them but the first mate certainly had.

"You heard what Captain Red said lads – put your backs into it! And that includes you, Reggae. Get that music OFF!"

"OK, Marcus," sighed a pirate with long dreadlocks, slowly removing his headset. "Go easy on us, can't you? We've been digging for treasure for months now – every single day - we're all done-in!"

"Yeah, Reggae is right!" muttered a hefty stern-looking pirate, with a silver stud in his left ear. "When we left Bristol HE says we'd be back home in eight WEEKS! That was eight MONTHS ago! It's not fair. Stuck in these scruffy pirate rags all day with no pay, no music and no phone!"

"Stop your whining, Benito!" barked the first mate. "You knew the score when you signed up. You answered the advert! Pirates from the 'Golden Age' didn't have no mobile phones or gadgets. They didn't wear designer jeans neither, so get used to it. It was your choice!"

Benito didn't reply, but after a few moments the pirate with dreadlocks started complaining again.

"Yeah, that be so Marcus, we did sign up, but not for 8 months! Scrubbing the decks, mending the sails, sword practice, pistol practice, canon drills - it's too much. We deserve a rest!"

"Don't you let the Captain hear you say such things, " warned the first mate, "or…"

"Or what?" scoffed Benito. "He'll make us walk the plank?"

The other pirates started to laugh.

"Who does he think he is?" mocked Benito, getting to his feet. "Black Beard's long-lost cousin?"

The other pirates laughed even louder.

"Just because he looks and talks like a pirate from long ago it don't mean he is one," continued Benito, with his hands on his hips. "He's just a normal bloke from Bristol – just a lot more crazy! He's no more a true pirate from the 'Golden Age' than the rest of us!"

* * *

"You're wrong!" snapped a girl-pirate, with short, red hair who seemed to appear from nowhere. "Trust me. I know his past! He is related to BLACKBEARD - one of the most frightening and notorious pirates that ever lived! You'd be a fool to cross him!"

"Yeah, missy and Usain Bolt's my little bro!" replied Benito, sarcastically. "Lady, you are so young and gullible!"

The other pirates roared with laughter.

"Don't you insult me, mister!" replied the girl-pirate crossly, pulling out her sword and waving it towards him. "I am telling you the truth!"

The pirates laughed even louder.

"Kat, the cabin-girl, knows him better than all of us, you'd best listen to her!" shouted the first mate firmly. "Now get digging, all of you - at once!"

The pirates followed their orders immediately... except for one! Benito sat back against our tree defiantly, shuffling his pack of cards.

"All we want is to just chill for a while, bro. Eat some coconut, lie in the sun, play some cards and listen to some reggae. Just chill – life's too short, bro..."

All of a sudden, Captain Red appeared from behind some trees and exploded into a fit of rage.

"MUTINY!" he bellowed, nostrils flared, eyes bulging. Benito sprang to his feet instantly and glanced fearfully towards the Captain.

"You idle, faint-hearted, yellow-bellied

traitor! You dare to mock the word of your Captain and doubt his bloodline?"

Benito suddenly looked petrified and started to mumble a few words of apology.

"Life is too short is it... BRO?" sneered the Captain, menacingly. "Well your life be about to get a lot shorter!"

The Captain threw the startled pirate to the ground and kicked up sand into his face. Benito coughed and spluttered but the Captain wasn't finished. He drew his long sword and thrust it towards the panic-stricken pirate, who was now squirming on his back like an upturned crab.

The first swipe missed his head by a few centimetres, but the second was even closer and the third! The Captain continued to swish his sword wildly, each time his helpless victim rolled frantically from side to side to avoid certain injury - blubbing and crying for mercy.

It was one of the scariest things I've ever seen, or ever want to see! But to my amazement, the pirate got up unscathed, apart from a slight cut to his right ear.

"Next time I'll cut your mutinous tongue clean out!" hissed the Captain, waving his sword in the air again, madly.

The Captain must have been an expert swordsman to miss him on purpose so many times. Maybe he really was related to that infamous pirate called Blackbeard? He certainly seemed scary enough.

"Does anyone else feel the same as he?" screeched the Captain sternly, eyeing-up his crew.

There was no reply. The crew looked scared stiff! We all were. My heart was beating faster than ever and so was Minoo's. I looked across at the others. Dad was comforting Sanjana and Mum had her eyes tightly closed.

"Let that be a lesson to you all!" continued the Captain, now standing high up on a rock, so he looked even taller and more terrifying than before.

"We be brave pirates! We be honorable pirates! We be loyal pirates, like the pirates of the 'Golden Age'. We fight for each other and die for each other!"

The pirates all cheered loudly, waving their swords and daggers in the air.

"Now back to work, you lazy land-lubbers! There is booty to be had for all of us!"

* * *

Chapter 12

Coconut Cannon-Fire!

The last few minutes had seemed like hours, but we were still alive and safe... for the moment anyway. We watched from high in the trees as the pirates set to work again. They worked in small groups and within half an hour they had dug four or five massive holes.

Each time a new hole was dug the Captain rushed over and looked in excitedly. Then he cursed angrily and walked away to the next.

"Scurvy dogs!" he snarled.

Suddenly I heard the Captain mumble a few words, one of which sounded like 'Zeo'. Maybe they were looking for 'The Lost Treasure of Zeo', but why here?

"Devil and doubloons!" grumbled Captain Red again loudly, as he peered into an empty hole.

Within half an hour our whole camp had been dug up. There must have been almost thirty holes. Captain Red looked at the map again and cursed.

"Confound this muddling map!" he yelled angrily, waving his sword in the air again wildly. "The treasure should be here! Bosh and hogwash! Cutlasses and cannon-fire!"

He was right under our tree now and he was looking meaner and nastier than any pirate I had ever seen in the movies. Through the coconut canopy, we could see his map quite clearly now and for some reason it looked strangely familiar. Suddenly I realised why! It was MY map!

MY MAP of the island!!!

The one I had made and put into the bottle the night before. The one with Zeo's Oasis and Giant Rock and a big cross to mark our camp. The pirates must have come across it this morning out at sea and now they must be thinking it is a TREASURE map! Now they must be thinking the big cross for our camp is Zeo's Treasure!!

"Oh no!" I gasped anxiously, to myself. "I've really done it this time. If Dad finds out he'll probably bury me alive in one of those holes!"

I looked over to Dad to find Sanjana whispering something into his ear. The next second Dad was glaring at me and I knew that he knew!

"You IDIOT!" he exploded, looking almost as angry as Captain Red.

But if I was an idiot, then so was Dad. He had forgotten the pirates were just below us! Most of the pirates looked up instantly and peered high into the trees.

"Did you hear that, Captain?" shrieked a skinny pirate with no teeth.

"Maybe the Black Pirates got here first?" shouted the first mate, suspiciously.

I held my breath and I'm sure the others did too. We couldn't afford to make a sound. Our only hope was to stay still and hope they couldn't see us. My heart pounded and I clung Minoo close to me...

Captain Red didn't reply. He stood motionless, eyes fixed on the tree where we were hidden – where we thought we were hidden…

"Can we go up after them, Captain and slit their throats?" demanded the skinny pirate, holding up his knife gleefully.

"Please!?" pleaded some of the others.

Suddenly a devilish smirk came over the Captain's face and in a slow, sinister voice he said, "No, let THEY come down to us!"

As he spoke he swished the blade of his sword into the base of our tree with tremendous force…

"WHACK!"

A huge chunk of the trunk splintered off and fell to the ground. A loud cheer went up from all the pirates. The force of the blow surprised us all and travelled all the way up the tree. We hung on for dear life. It felt like an earthquake!

The pirates laughed and cheered as Captain Red swung his sword again and again into the bottom of our tree.

"WHACK!"
"WHACK!"
"WHACK!"

Things looked very, very bad indeed! The trunk was thick, but it wouldn't last much longer...

But before the Captain had time to land another blow, a giant coconut came hurtling down from our tree and landed smack on top of his head! The Captain groaned in agony and slumped to the ground in a heap. Minoo had come to the rescue! What a shot!

Almost immediately some of Minoo's monkey friends joined in and soon there was a heavy bombardment of coconuts pounding down on the pirates, just like a volley of cannon fire!

I thought the pirates had looked fierce and mean, but they weren't acting like it now.

"Ouch!" cried one, as he took a direct hit to his nose.

"Mama!" yelled another, jumping into a hole for cover.

The pirates were all in a panic! Soon they were scampering and scurrying for cover in all directions but there was no escape - the coconuts kept coming!

Captain Red was livid! He stood defiantly in the open, with his first mate close by his side, his face red with rage.

"Yellow-bellied scurvy dogs!" he bellowed furiously, "Return to your posts, men!"

"And women!" replied Kat the cabin-girl, proudly taking her place by his side.

The pirates reluctantly came out of their hiding places and looked towards our tree nervously, in fear of the next volley of coconuts.

"Return fire, at once!" barked Captain Red, angrily.

The pirates carried out their orders and suddenly we were the ones under attack. Rocks and coconuts came hurtling towards us and fired past our ears like cannon balls!

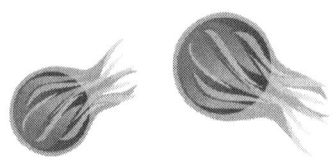

We all hung on tightly and prayed the rocks and coconuts would miss us. If we were hit – that would be it – we were 'goners'! Our cover would be blown. Either they would hear our cries of pain or worse... see us plummeting headfirst out of the tree! We had to do something and quick!

But what...?

Suddenly Minoo jumped out of our tree and swung along the upper canopy to another group of taller trees some twenty metres away.

Minoo's monkey friends followed his lead and soon they were pounding the pirates with coconuts from their new position - well away from our tree. We were safe! Minoo had succeeded in drawing their fire!

"It's just a troop of wild monkeys up there, Captain!" cried the cabin-girl, ducking to just avoid another air-borne missile.

"I think you be right," replied the Captain, taking another hit to the chest. "Bothersome pests!"

"Shall I give them the taste of our fire power?" asked the skinny pirate eagerly, pointing his old-fashioned pistol in the air.

"No privateer," ordered the Captain firmly, turning towards the shore. "Don't go wasting your powder on mischievous monkeys. We will save it for the Black Pirates. Now, let's be off! There be no treasure for us here but I'll wager that the Black Pirates are not far away and they be knowing where the booty is hidden!"

We watched nervously as the pirates returned back to their ship and only when we saw it disappear out to sea did we dare come down from our hiding place.

We couldn't believe our luck, Minoo and his friends had saved us all. What a hero he was! We all sang 'three cheers' for him and his friends and Mum and Dad found them some extra treats to eat from the store.

Unfortunately, Dad wasn't so impressed with me.

"Your daft map could have cost us our lives! How on earth did the pirates get hold of it?"

Reluctantly, I explained what had happened. The map, the bottle, everything.

"What a crazy idea!" sighed Dad. "You just don't think."

"You're one to talk!" cried Mum, staring at Dad in amazement. "You didn't THINK when we were high up in the tree! Your booming voice put the pirates right onto us. We were lucky to escape with our lives!"

Dad went quiet for a few seconds and started to look very uncomfortable.

"Mum's right, it was a stupid thing to do. I don't know what I was thinking..."

"At least we are all safe now. That's the main thing," interrupted Mum cheerfully.

"Yes we are, thank goodness," agreed Dad, apologetically, ruffling my hair with his hand. "It was quick thinking to get us to hide up the tree. Well done, Jay! It saved us all."

Mum went round giving us all gigantic hugs and telling us how much she loved us, and how she was so scared she was going to lose us.

We told her we felt the same and then Sanjana said she was ten times more scared of being high up than she was of the 'panicky pirates'. We all laughed together and started to impersonate the pirates running away from the coconut bombardment.

"Help!" cried Sanjana, in her best pirate voice. "It's a troop of wild monkeys! Help, Mama! Help!"

Then Dad suddenly went into action mode again.

"They'll be no Coconut Surprise for you tonight, young man, until you sort out this lot!" Dad was pointing at the holes all around our camp.

"It was your map that caused all this mess, so you'd better get on with it, right now!"

Things felt back to normal.

As Minoo and his monkey friends helped me move the earth back into the holes, little did I know that something amazing was soon to happen...

* * *

Chapter 13

Treasure

I told you something amazing was about to happen, and the very next day when I was playing hide-and-seek with Minoo, it did!

I was hiding from Minoo in a brilliant spot I had found, actually IN Takootu Falls. Just behind the cascading waters there was a small cave. I'd got a bit wet getting there, but it was worth it; Minoo would never find me!

Water was gushing down from above and the sun lit up the small cave with bright rainbow colours dancing all over the walls. Suddenly I noticed a small wooden box in the corner of the cave. It looked very old and it had strange markings on it, a bit like the ones I had seen on Takootu's boat. I opened it up to find a scroll of paper tied with a piece of red ribbon. This looked interesting I thought! I pushed the ribbon off excitedly and rolled out the paper carefully, so I could see what it was. It looked like a map of an island!

The markings were quite faint and the writing was small and old-fashioned, so I held it up to the sunlight to get a better view. I could see things more clearly now and could just make out what some of the bigger words said. The first word I recognised was 'ZEO' and the second word I could see clearly was 'TREASURE'! Then I noticed a black cross and by it was a small sketch of a chest – a treasure chest!

I couldn't believe my eyes! It was a treasure map. A REAL treasure map! Zeo's Treasure! The treasure Takootu had told us about. I had found the map for the Lost Treasure of Zeo!

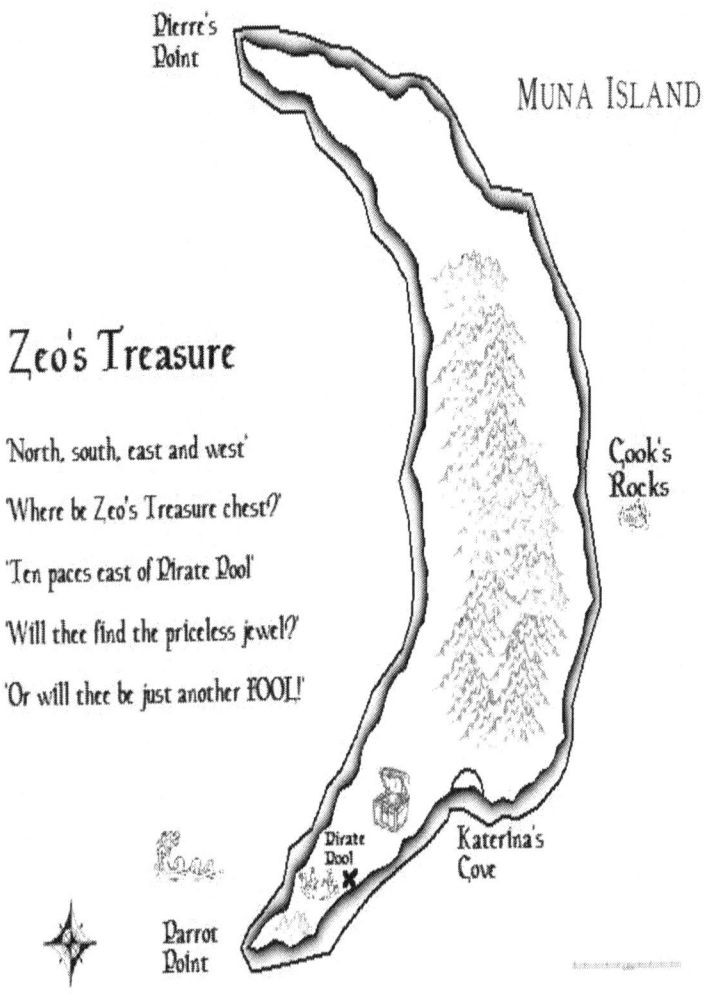

Pierre's
Point

MUNA ISLAND

Zeo's Treasure

'North, south, east and west'

'Where be Zeo's Treasure chest?'

'Ten paces east of Pirate Pool'

'Will thee find the priceless jewel?'

'Or will thee be just another FOOL!'

Cook's
Rocks

Pirate
Pool

Katerina's
Cove

Parrot
Point

I ran back in a daze to tell the others and was so excited I went straight through a patch of Prickly-Pong. I arrived back smelling disgusting, but it didn't seem to upset anyone. They were too interested in the map to notice!

"It looks like Muna Island!" cried Dad eagerly, examining the map. "I remember Takootu pointing it out on the day we arrived. It's not far away."

"What a hero!" beamed Mum, giving me a high-five.

"The Lost Treasure of Zeo! How amazing!" shouted Sanjana. "Look! I think there's some sort of riddle to help us find it..."

"I can't wait to tell Takootu!" I said, jumping in the air with excitement.

Minoo looked happy too. He was jumping up and down and chattering even more than usual.

Suddenly I was the most popular person on the island! Everyone was being so friendly and nice. Mum declared a two-day school holiday, Dad played coconut cricket with me (and let me win!) and Sanjana did all the washing-up, even though it was my turn. It felt good to be popular for a change.

Later that evening, after my fifth 'Coconut Surprise', we settled down with the map to make a plan. A plan to find and rescue the 'Lost Treasure of Zeo'.

Chapter 14

The Choice

The plan was quite simple. Build a raft and sail to Muna Island to get the treasure. Dad had been building boats as a hobby from when he was a boy. His grandad had taught him and they had made several voyages to the Isle of Wight in the long summer holidays. According to Dad, Muna island was very close. He remembered seeing it on the way – in fact we could see it from Giant Rock!

Unfortunately there was a problem. The wood we needed for the raft meant we would have to cut down some of the giant palms. Mum, Dad and Sanjana didn't seem to mind, but I wasn't sure. The trees were part of the island and

Minoo and his friends lived in them. Takootu had told us to look after the island and so had Grandad. There must be some other way, surely?

"What do you think we should do then, Jay?" joked Dad. "Build a raft out of sea-weed and Prickly-Pong!"

The others laughed but I didn't think it was very funny.

"We could wait for Takootu to come, he's got a boat and will know where to go. Why don't we just wait for Takootu?"

"Jay's right," said Mum. "It would make it a lot easier. We wouldn't have to build a boat and cut down any trees. It would be safer for us too. How do we know the raft won't sink!?"

Dad reminded Mum that he had been building rafts and boats since he was a teenager.

"Anyway," he added, starting to get

impatient. "Takootu isn't coming for another few weeks. Someone else might find the treasure in that time. Like that crazy Captain Red! I think we should get on with it now."

There was a long discussion. Sanjana agreed with Dad and eventually so did Mum. I was the only one who wanted to wait for Takootu, but I was out-voted.

"I want to find the treasure too, you know!" I protested, feeling a bit upset with the others. "But how would you like it if someone came and chopped our house down?"

"Oh don't get so sentimental, Jay." moaned Dad. "We'll only be using a few trees. I doubt if Minoo will even notice they've gone."

Somehow I didn't think that would be true, but I wasn't sure. Maybe I was getting upset about nothing. Maybe a few trees wouldn't hurt? Perhaps Minoo wouldn't notice after all?

We were wrong. Minoo noticed all right and Dad noticed him too, and more to the point what he was throwing - great big coconuts! It was just like with the pirates, as soon as Dad started to chop down the first tree... BANG! A giant coconut hit him smack on the head!

Dad was dazed for a few seconds and stumbled to the ground. I knew how hard those coconuts were and ran over to see how he was. I offered him the 'magic' yellow plant to relieve his pain.

"Don't fuss, Jay, it's only a bump! I've had a lot worse playing rugby." groaned Dad.

I could see he was hurt but he didn't want to show it. Dad looked angry and even more determined to carry on with his plan. That evening he made himself a protective helmet out of a hollowed-out coconut with red seaweed for padding and he returned in the morning to the 'battle zone'.

A few minutes later he was chopping away and the coconuts were firing past his ears like cricket balls! But Dad just kept chopping. The first tree fell with a crash to the ground and was soon followed by another and another. Minoo looked on sadly.

Within an hour, Dad had enough wood to start building and by the next afternoon the raft was ready to set sail! We were all really excited and watched on eagerly.

Unfortunately, the launch didn't go well. 'Smith 1' was hit by a huge wave, as it passed the reef and split into pieces! Dad swam back to shore and trudged back up the beach looking sodden and miserable.

"I thought you said you were an expert?" teased Sanjana.

Dad pulled a face and carried on up the beach. Minoo looked on gleefully and the giant green parrots seemed to squawk with laughter.

Dad didn't see the funny side though and started to talk about a new one straight away.

"I need to make this one more streamlined," he said enthusiastically, "so it will cut through the waves. But I need more help!"

Back at camp Dad told us his plan but

I was still concerned about Minoo and his trees.

"Stop fussing, Jay!" muttered Dad, impatiently. "There's still a whole forest of palm trees on the island!"

"But there won't be if we keep cutting them all down!"

The island wasn't that big and you could notice the difference already.

"I think we should wait for Takootu to come. He's got a good boat and he knows all the islands well. Why don't we just wait for Takootu?"

"Let's not have that discussion all over again please, Jay," said Dad, trying to stay patient. "We want to find the treasure FIRST – remember!"

It was true, we did all want to find the treasure first, so there seemed no other choice but to build another raft. Dad asked me to keep Minoo out of the way so he could get on in peace, without having to dodge flying coconuts. I reluctantly agreed and spent the next couple of afternoons playing coconut cricket, football and hide-and-seek with Minoo and his friends on the other side of the island.

It made me feel a little awkward and guilty. While we were playing, Dad was cutting down more trees - Minoo's home! I'm sure Minoo knew what was going on, but he still seemed as friendly as ever.

In the evenings, I helped Dad and the others build the raft. Hopefully, this one would be a success and we wouldn't need to cut down any more trees.

* * *

By the end of the week 'Smith 2' was finished. It was bigger and stronger, but sadly it didn't do much better than the first. It crashed into a hidden reef a few metres from the shore and started to break in two.

The monkeys seemed to be laughing, as Dad stomped moodily back to camp, but I wasn't. Dad was going to have to build another raft now and that meant more trees were going to be destroyed!

"Stop whining, Jay!" snapped Dad, "There are still plenty of trees left."

"But that's not all I'm bothered about, Dad!" I shouted, suddenly getting into a panic. "Look!"

I pointed to a spot where the first few trees had been cut down. Only the stumps remained now and around them was a mass of Prickly-Pong, which seemed to be a lot TALLER than it had been before!

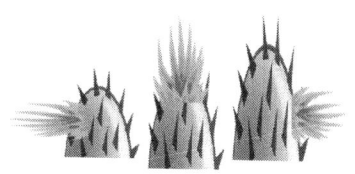

Minoo had noticed it too and was now waving a stick wildly around his head, as though he was trying to scare the Prickly-Pong away.

"It's getting bigger!" I cried. "If we cut any more trees down it might get out of control!"

"Don't talk nonsense, Jay!" sighed Dad. "It looks exactly the same height to me."

"If anything it looks smaller," sneered Sanjana.

"You really must stop imagining things, Jay," said Mum, in her teacher voice. "We know you want to save the trees but there's no need to make up stories!"

"I'm not making up stories!" I protested angrily. "It's taller! I'm sure it is!"

"I think you need to rest in the shade for a while, Jay Jackson Smith. You have obviously been out in the sun far too long – it's playing tricks with your eyes!" added Dad, annoyingly.

The sun was hot but there was nothing wrong with my eyesight, or Minoo's and I was determined to prove it. But how? If only I had some evidence they would have to believe me. Maybe I could get some...

* * *

Chapter 15

The Test

I rushed back to camp and rummaged through Dad's tool box until I found what I was looking for - his metal ruler! It was just what I wanted and I set to work straight away.

I started to measure how high the Prickly-Pong was in 2 different places around the island. Half of the measurements were under trees that had been cut down and the other half was where the trees hadn't been cut down. Minoo helped me hold the ruler straight and I recorded the measurements in my notebook. I felt like a real scientist!

I remember my teacher, Mrs Jones

telling us you needed to make lots of readings to help make the results more reliable.

'More readings, make results more reliable.'

That's what she always taught us, so we kept on measuring!

After thirty measurements, fifteen in each place, we stopped and climbed up Giant Rock to rest and look at the results more closely. I looked carefully at the heights to see if there was a pattern and could hardly believe it. They were astonishing!

Height of Prickly-Pong (tall tree)

2 cm	5 cm	4 cm	6 cm	5cm
4 cm	6 cm	7 cm	8 cm	2 cm
5 cm	4cm	7 cm	3 cm	7 cm

The tallest Prickly-Pong under the Giant palm trees was 8 cm high, which was only just about level with my ankle. But the tallest Prickly-Pong plant, where the trees had been cut down, was now 58 cm high! Even I could work out the difference in height was 50 cm. That was half a metre! That meant the Prickly-Pong really WAS getting taller...

A lot, lot TALLER!!!!

What's more, if it could grow 50 cm taller in a matter of days, how high would it be after a few weeks, months or years? The thought of the damage the 'Giant' Prickly-Pong could do to the island scared me stiff, so I rushed back to tell the others.

"So that's where my ruler got to!" snapped Dad, yanking it out of my hand.

"Yes," I cried urgently. "But what about the Prickly-Pong?"

Mum and Dad glanced casually at the results in my notebook and then started to talk about standard deviation and fair tests and other words I didn't really understand. Then they said that it didn't prove anything and that you couldn't trust statistics.

But I knew what they were really saying. They didn't believe me or maybe they just didn't want to believe me, because then they would have to stop cutting the trees down.

"Don't you see!" I cried, in one last desperate attempt to convince them. "It's the light! The Prickly-Pong is growing taller because it's getting more light!"

"Light isn't the only thing that plants need in order to grow," said Dad dismissively.

"Light is very important though," said Sanjana, confidently. "We did it in science this year with Mrs Jones. She said that plants growing in the shade of trees are often prevented from growing taller because they don't get enough light. And there is also a lack of space and water. Simple really!"

I couldn't believe it! Finding the treasure map had been a surprise, but having 'super-smart' Sanjana on MY side was unbelievable! It made me feel quite uneasy and Dad wasn't looking too happy either.

"All right," said Dad, defensively. "Maybe you have a point. Maybe the

Prickly-Pong is getting a little taller. So what? It can't hurt us! It's a little plant."

"I'm not so sure," continued Sanjana, suddenly looking extremely serious. "Mrs Jones said that if the ecological balance was upset by man, it could cause a change in the relative dominance of a particular species, which could be catastrophic!"

"Yes!" I shouted in agreement, not having a clue what Sanjana was going on about. "It's dangerous! Really dangerous! The Prickly-Pong is getting out of control!"

"The only thing getting out of control around here, are your imaginations!" shouted Dad, angrily. "Now beat it, the pair of you. Before I lose my temper!"

We knew we were right about the Prickly-Pong and so we decided to try and do something about it ourselves. We got some spades and heavy sticks from our camp and started to beat and bash down the biggest Prickly-Pong plants. Minoo helped and Sanjana did too, but it didn't have much effect.

Next we tried to cut the plants off at the stem with the saw and a sharp knife, but the stems were so thick and prickly it was difficult to cut through them. It took us about half an hour to cut down just THREE plants! We kept going though, we were determined to do something, but by sun-set there were still masses of the BIG Prickly-Pong plants left.

Sanjana had worked really hard and now had several nasty scratches all over her hands and arms, in fact we all did. We sat down by Takootu Falls exhausted and dressed our wounds with the magic fruit which I named 'Prickly-Gone'.

"Thanks for helping, Sanjana. You were brilliant!"

"Thanks Jay, so were you and Minoo. But it hasn't made much difference has it?" replied Sanjana, wearily.

We would try again tomorrow but we knew deep down that we were beaten – there were just too many plants.

Minoo snuggled up on my lap and chewed on a piece of coconut. I could sense he was feeling scared about his home. I was too.

"If only I was Captain Red," I said to Minoo and Sanjana dejectedly, "I'd make Mum and Dad walk the plank or sit on a BIG Prickly-Pong! They'd listen to us then!"

Chapter 16

The Voyage

Unfortunately, the next day it was us who were walking the plank; slightly reluctantly onto the deck of 'Smith 3'. Dad had successfully tested the new craft in the morning and so the hunt for the Lost Treasure of Zeo was now on!

Dad had done an excellent job with finishing it and it looked more like a small boat than a raft. It had a proper sail which could be moved left and right depending on the wind, and it even had a rudder.

"Get these on!" shouted Dad, throwing us a life-jacket each. "I thought they would come in handy."

Although I was really excited at the thought of finding the treasure, I couldn't stop thinking about what was happening to our island and what might happen to Minoo and his friends.

"What about the Prickly-Pong?" I demanded. "And Minoo! I want Minoo to come with us!"

"Just get on, please," shouted Dad impatiently. "I'm not having HIM on board!"

Dad still hadn't forgiven Minoo for all the coconuts he had thrown at him. I felt uneasy. I had a strange feeling that something terrible was going to happen.

I waved to Minoo, who was perched high up in one of his favourite trees and he waved back uncertainly. He looked sad and scared. Maybe he thought I was leaving the island for good or maybe he was just worried about the Prickly-Pong.

"Be careful!" I cried out, as our boat set sail. "Be careful, Minoo. We'll be back soon!"

The sea was calm and there was a steady breeze behind us. Dad was in charge of the sail and he barked out orders to us all, like we were competitors in an Olympic yacht race!

The sun was shining brightly and blue dolphins jumped playfully close to our boat. What a beautiful place we lived in.

* * *

"Land ahoy!" shouted Mum excitedly pointing to a sandy shore in the distance.

"Is it Muna Island?" asked Sanjana eagerly.

"Yes!" shouted Dad, smiling. "I told you it wasn't far."

"Muna Island, Jay!" cried Sanjana very excitedly. "MUNA Island!"

"Hopefully, TREASURE Island!" I

replied, cheerfully, peering through my telescope to get a closer look.

I could see a few palm trees, but not as many as on our island and there were masses of hills to the north.

We were all feeling incredibly excited. The search for the Lost Treasure of Zeo was about to begin!

We landed at what we thought was Parrot Point. It certainly was a very narrow piece of land, but we couldn't see any parrots around. Dad had now taken charge of the treasure map and he was convinced this was the best place to start looking.

Sanjana and I started to chant the riddle from the map, which we had learnt off by heart.

"North, south, east and west!
Where be Zeo's Treasure chest?
Ten paces east of Pirate Pool.
Will thee find the priceless jewel?
Or will thee be just another FOOL!"

According to the riddle, Zeo's Treasure was hidden ten paces east of Pirate Pool, so all we had to do was find Pirate Pool and we would be almost there!

Unfortunately, it didn't turn out as simple as that. We searched and searched for more than two hours, but none of us set eyes on a puddle let alone a pool.

"This must be Pierre's Point, not Parrot Point," said Sanjana, pushing the map under Dad's nose. "I thought you said you could read a map!"

Dad looked slightly embarrassed and made some excuse about not having his reading glasses.

We were at the wrong end of the island! No wonder we couldn't find Pirate Pool.

We all got back onto the 'Smith 3' and sailed south along a rocky coastline, past Katerina's Cave and landed at Parrot Point. Well we hoped it was Parrot Point this time! We were all feeling exhausted and it was getting dark, so we decided to make camp for the night.

* * *

Chapter 17

Zeo's Treasure

The next morning, Sanjana and I were so excited we woke up early – just like at Christmas! After a quick breakfast, we set off to find the treasure. We chanted Zeo's riddle together happily, as we searched in the early morning sunlight.

"North, south, east and west!
Where be Zeo's Treasure Chest?
Ten paces east of Pirate Pool.
Will thee find the priceless jewel?
Or will thee be - just another FOOL?"

We hadn't been searching for long when we saw what we were looking for.

"There!" I shouted loudly, to the others.

"Down on the right!"

We sprinted down the hill eagerly, but as we got closer we couldn't quite believe the view. There wasn't just one pool, like it said in the riddle, there must have been at least five. All different shapes and sizes!

"Which ONE is Pirate Pool?" sighed Mum despondently.

"I don't know," replied Dad, gloomily. "On the map it only shows one!"

"Maybe there was only one pool originally," explained Sanjana. "But over the years it has dried up and split into smaller ones. We did something like it in geography last year."

"Maybe we ARE all going to look like FOOLS – like the riddle warned us!" said Mum, dejectedly.

"Yes, this is going to take a lot longer than we thought," sighed Dad, getting out his spade. "So let's get started!"

I suggested that we start digging east of the biggest pond and to my surprise the others all agreed. For the next six days it felt like we spent every second of every minute of every hour DIGGING! Dig! Dig! Dig! That's all we did! We must have dug over a hundred holes between us, but still there was no sign of the treasure.

'Ten paces east of Pirate Pool' might sound like a simple instruction, but that's assuming there is only ONE pool, and that your paces are the same size as the person who buried it and that you start measuring your paces from the same place as they did.

Our backs were aching, our hands were covered in blisters and I was starting to regret ever finding the stupid treasure map!

"I don't get it," moaned Dad, unhappily throwing his spade to the ground. "We have now dug ten paces east of all five pools and still... NOTHING!"

Dad was right, we had followed the riddle to the letter! It didn't make any sense, unless, unless.... suddenly I had an idea!

Maybe, just maybe, the person who drew the map and wrote the riddle had made a mistake like I had, when I had made my map of Gigantuki Island. Maybe they got things mixed up like me? Like their east and west? Or maybe they had done it on purpose to make it impossible to find and make us all look like FOOLS?

While the others were having a lunch break I ran over to the other side of the biggest pool – the WEST side (not the east) and counted out ten paces. Then I stopped and counted out another ten paces. I knew my pace was exactly half of Dad's, so twenty of mine were the same as ten of his.

Then I started digging. Although I was exhausted I seemed to be digging with new energy and within half-an-hour I had dug a huge hole. Sadly, there was still no sign of treasure. I carried on for another hour or so, but still there was nothing. Maybe I had got it wrong? Maybe I was letting my imagination run away with me?

I was getting tired now and I was just about to stop and move onto the next pool, when suddenly my spade hit something hard... It sounded like metal! My heart missed a beat. Could this be it? I scraped the earth away as fast as I could and then stared downwards in shock... There it was! A dark, rusty old chest! I took my spade and swung it at the lock... CRASH! The lock fell open...

My heart was racing now and I shouted to the others for help. I tried to open the lid but it was stuck solid. I couldn't budge it! So I wedged the blade of my spade into a narrow opening and pushed down on the handle as hard as I could. Slowly but surely the lid started to open wider and wider, until I could just get a glimpse of what was inside...

I couldn't believe my eyes and neither could the others who had just arrived at the scene. Sanjana helped me push the lid completely open and then we all gasped in amazement!

The chest was full of the most exotic looking jewels in the world! Sparkling white diamonds, deep red rubies, shimmering green emeralds and shiny black pearls! All covered by hundreds and hundreds of gold doubloons.

"You're a genius!" cried Dad, whose eyes looked like they were about to pop right out of their sockets. "A born genius!"

No one had ever called me that. Then everyone went crazy. Dad did a cartwheel, Mum danced into the pool with all her clothes on and 'Silly Sanjana' tried to kiss me - AND I let her!

After a while, we all calmed down and started the short walk back to the boat. The treasure was extremely heavy and we all had to take turns in helping Dad to carry it. It took us a while, but we got back to the boat and loaded the chest on carefully. We didn't want the boat to sink.

We were just about to set sail when we all got the biggest shock of our lives!

"Not so fast!" came a threatening, west-country voice. "What have we here?"

We turned around, trembling and there, not ten metres away, stood Captain Red and his pirates. We were done for!

"I was guessing there was someone else living on Gigantuki Island besides those crazy, wild monkeys," boasted Captain Red, looking us up and down. "And it looks like I be right!"

"It's treasure, Captain!" cried the skinny pirate with no teeth, peering into the chest.

"Of course it's treasure you chump!" blasted the Captain, eyes bulging with menace.

Then he walked slowly towards us and whispered slyly.

"But whose treasure is it? Eh? It certainly isn't yours. I be thinking it might be Zeo's Treasure. Am I right?"

We were all too scared to say anything and just stood there silently, trembling with fear.

"Spit it out, strangers from Gigantuki Island!" threatened Captain Red angrily, as he drew his long menacing sword from his belt. "I'm not a man who likes to be kept waiting. I'll count to three! One, two..."

"Yes, it's Zeo's Treasure!" shouted Mum desperately, "Take it, it's yours! But please don't hurt us. Please!"

"I knew it!" Captain Red cried triumphantly, slapping the first mate on the back in celebration. "But do not distress yourself lady. We have no reason to hurt you. All we want is what do belong to us. Nothing more - nothing less!"

"But it doesn't belong to you!" I suddenly blurted out, not really thinking what I was doing. "It belongs to the people of Radimatu."

Captain Red looked mildly shocked at my outburst and then laughed in a sinister manner.

"Such boldness in a young sprat! Commendable, very commendable... I could do with someone courageous like you on my ship. Most of my crew are half-wits or cowards!"

"Don't say another word, Jay," whispered Mum. "He's dangerous!"

"But although you are brave, my boy," he continued, "you are a fool to try and cross Captain Red. Zeo's Treasure belongs to me. The only living survivor of the 'Bandi', NOT the chosen few from Radimatu!"

The Captain looked angrier than he ever had – eyes bulging, nostrils flaring – he looked mad!

"So, strangers from Gigantuki Island, hand it over... NOW! Or you will all be walking the PLANK! The sharks are looking especially hungry today, don't you think?"

The pirates laughed and jeered loudly. There was no way we wanted to be fed to the sharks and were just about to unload the treasure chest, when we suddenly noticed strange men in canoes racing across the bay towards us!

They were dressed all in black, in what seemed like traditional Tahitian dress, like warriors from long ago. They were heavily tattooed and looked stern and strong.

* * *

"It's the Black Pirates!" cried one of Captain Red's men, sounding startled.

Captain Red looked out over the bay and cursed.

"Scurvy-dogs! Quick! To the beach!" he bellowed, waving his sword wildly above his head. "Fight bravely crew, like the pirates from the Golden Age! With honour and valour and the booty shall soon be ours!"

The Black Pirates were just landing on the shore about fifty metres north of us. There must have been about twenty of them and they were all carrying long sticks and spear-like weapons.

Soon they were racing up the beach towards Captain Red and his men. Meanwhile, Captain Red and his men were sprinting down the beach towards them. Within a matter of seconds, there was a brutal brawl of a battle going on...

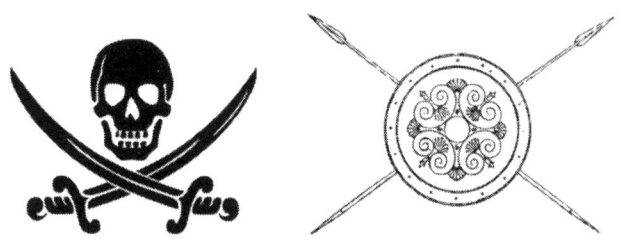

While the pirates were busy fighting we took our chance! It was now or never - we had to try to escape...

Dad carefully pushed 'Smith 3' away from the shore and jumped in, ever so quietly, not daring to make a sound. We were moving east along the coast, away from the raging battle. I couldn't bear to look back at the pirates fighting. I just looked straight ahead and listened...

Listened for the cries of anger when they realised that we were escaping. Listened for the sound of Captain Red's menacing voice yelling at his crew, from his chasing ship. Listened for the boom of a cannon being fired to halt our escape...

But to my amazement and relief there was nothing!

All I could hear was the battle cries of pirates fighting. Shrieks and yells - moans and groans – heckling and hissing!

As time passed, the cries grew softer and softer until eventually they disappeared completely.

Suddenly I realised that we were out in

the open sea. I looked back and all I could see was Muna island in the distance and there was nobody coming after us. We had escaped! We were safe! Safe for the moment anyway...

Maybe I would get a chance to eat Grandma's flapjack again after all?

* * *

Chapter 18

Prickly-Pong Island

On the voyage back we were all feeling incredibly relieved. We knew the pirates might come after us but we prayed that they wouldn't.

Finding the treasure and escaping from the pirates had somehow brought us closer together. Soon we were all laughing and joking and discussing what we should do with it all.

Dad wanted it to help him start a new design business, Mum wanted to buy her own art studio and Sanjana wanted to go on a massive shopping trip to New York. I wanted to buy my own island for Minoo and my friends to play on – where there would definitely be no schools allowed!

Then suddenly I thought about Takootu and his tribe - it was his treasure not ours!

"I think we should give it back to Takootu and his people," I said excitedly. "It's Zeo's Treasure! It's part of their history!"

There was a long silence. Everyone looked shocked at my suggestion, but after a few moments Mum and Sanjana agreed.

"Maybe we could keep just one small piece each as a souvenir?" said Mum, eyeing up a beautiful emerald necklace.

"Yes!" agreed Sanjana, "Maybe two or three?"

Dad didn't seem as keen on my idea though.

"It's a really nice thought, Jay, but just

think of all the money we could..."

Dad suddenly stopped in mid-sentence and stared ahead with an expression of shock and horror all rolled into one.

We all turned sharply, to see what he was looking at and could hardly believe our eyes...

It was our island! Gigantuki island, but it didn't look like the Gigantuki island we had left just days before. But we knew what we could see was real because it was the very thing we had feared might happen...

Our beautiful island had turned into a wild jungle of GIANT Prickly-Pong!

It was taller than the giant palms and was now engulfing the entire island!
Our beautiful, green shimmering palm trees were now looking sickly and weak. The giant Prickly-Pong, wrapped tightly around their slender trunks, seemed to have strangled the

life right out of them! The once tiny thorns were now the size of small swords, sticking out like daggers - threatening the sky. The crystal-clear waterfall flowing at Takootu Falls had turned dark purple and the horrific stench coming from the huge red flowers was indescribable.

Our beautiful home was no more, this was now...

Prickly-Pong Island!

The only place still visible was the very top of Giant Rock. On it stood some non-flying birds and parrots and several monkeys, but Minoo wasn't among them. Minoo was nowhere to be seen! I gazed agonisingly through my telescope, but there was no sign of him anywhere.

"Minoo! Minoo!" I called anxiously from the boat, as we got closer to shore. "We're back! It's me!"

There was no reply. Not even a chatter. There was an eerie silence. No monkeys chattering, no parrots squawking – just the sound of the waves lapping the shore.

"I'm so sorry, Jay!" said Mum, with tears streaming down her face. "You were right about the Prickly-Pong, I wish we had believed you."

Then Dad started to apologise and said it was all his fault, but his words didn't seem to make any sense. It didn't matter anymore. All I could think about was Minoo and where he had gone to. I kept on shouting his name, over and over again, but still there was no reply...

It was all my fault. I should never have left him on his own.

* * *

Chapter 19

Minoo

I wanted to get out and look for him but Dad said it was too dangerous on the island now, but I didn't care. I jumped out of the boat and sprinted up the beach towards our camp, calling Minoo's name as I ran.

The Prickly-Pong was so tall and thick it was impossible to move freely. Everywhere I turned it was there! It was like a maze of barbed wire. I could feel giant thorns cutting into my skin like a sharp knife, but although it hurt I kept going, I had to keep going. Minoo could be injured or trapped somewhere. I had to find him and fast!

Eventually I got to our tree-house, but there was no sign of him anywhere. After a moments rest I made my way back to Takootu Falls, covered in cuts and feeling scared and exhausted. I really needed a drink, but the water was now purple and poisoned.

I sat on a rock despondently, scary thoughts racing through my brain. Why had I left him on his own? How long could he survive in a dangerous place like this? Where would he try to hide? Was he still alive...?! I was scared, really scared. What if Minoo was... I should never have left him on his own!

"Where are you, Minoo!?" I shouted out desperately. **"Minoo! Minoo!!"**

There was no reply, but I kept calling. Minutes that seemed like hours passed by and still there was nothing. I was starting to give up hope of ever seeing Minoo again, when all of a sudden, I thought I heard a faint whimpering sound coming from near the waterfall.

Suddenly I had an idea! I quickly dodged through the flow of foul-smelling water and climbed into the secret cave, where I had found the treasure map a few weeks earlier. And there, sitting in the corner was an orangey, brown furry animal! It was covered in cuts and gashes and blood trickled from its wounds, but I recognised him at once. It was Minoo! He was alive!

His eyes lit up when he saw me and he started chattering, but not in his usual way. I could tell he was weak and not his usual self so I picked him up carefully in my arms and gave him a little hug.

"I'm sorry!" I whispered quietly, "I'm sorry for everything and for leaving you here. I'll never leave you again."

I carried Minoo down to the beach, where Mum and the others were waiting and looking worried. They seemed almost as pleased to see me as I was to find Minoo.

"Thank goodness you are safe!" cried Mum emotionally "We were all so worried!"

"I couldn't just leave him," I explained.

"We understand," said Dad, looking more upset than I had ever seen him. "You are a very brave and loyal friend. Minoo is lucky to have you."

"And I am lucky to have him!" I smiled.

After a big hugging session, Mum helped me bathe Minoo's wounds in salt water and some 'Prickly-Gone' that we found growing near the beach. Soon he was looking a little chirpier and more like the Minoo we knew, but he was still not right. I could tell from the way Mum was talking that she was worried about him and that made me even more concerned. I couldn't bear to think of Minoo dying.

"What are we going to do now?" asked Sanjana, anxiously. "We can't live here. Not now!"

"And nor can the animals!" I replied, sadly.

After a quick discussion, it was decided that there was only one thing we could do. We would go to a new island and take the monkeys and parrots with us.

We got back on to 'Smith 3' and sailed as close as we could to Giant Rock, where all the animals were marooned. Mum stayed in the boat with Minoo while the rest of us climbed up to the top. Carefully, we carried the parrots and non-flying birds back down to the boat. They were badly cut and too weak to struggle. The monkeys were injured too, but most of them managed to climb down on their own.

Minoo was so tired he didn't even notice them as we helped them onto 'Smith 3'. But just as we all got back on the boat something terrible happened. It started to...

SINK!

It couldn't take all our weight!

Dad and I jumped out immediately and the boat bobbed back up to its normal level. The boat wasn't strong enough to take us all and the treasure.

What were we going to do...?!

* * *

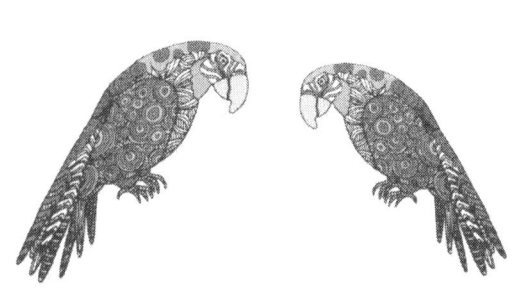

Chapter 20

The Emerald Treasure

"We'll have to leave the animals behind," said Dad, quietly. "It's the only way."

"No we won't!" cried Mum passionately, pointing to the treasure chest. "We can leave THAT behind instead!"

"The treasure?" replied Dad in astonishment.

"No, not the treasure, we've destroyed that! Our beautiful island – our beautiful 'emerald treasure' - is no more! And what for? A dirty old trunk full of metal and stones!"

Dad looked slightly confused, but after a few moments he seemed to understand what Mum was saying. He looked down at the treasure chest guiltily and then back towards the menacing jungle of Prickly-Pong.

"Mum's right," he replied, softly. "We have destroyed this beautiful green island, and for what?"

Dad looked back down at the old chest, uncomfortably. "It's up to you, Jay. You found it, it's your choice."

As far as I was concerned, there was no choice. The animals, and especially Minoo, were much more important and Sanjana completely agreed.

But Zeo's treasure was important to Takootu because it meant so much to him and his people. Suddenly, I had an idea!

"We can hide the chest in my secret cave, so Takootu can have it!" I cried, feeling a little more positive. "It should be safe there, until he returns."

The others all agreed that it was the best thing we could do, so Dad and Sanjana helped me move the treasure carefully into the cave. We were just on our way back to our boat, when mum suddenly cried out and started pointing towards the sea.

We gazed along the shore, fearing the worst, but it wasn't the pirates we could see... it was Takootu! There was Takootu smiling and waving to us from the 'Captain Cook'! He had returned!

"Thank goodness you is safe, family Smith!" cried Takootu cheerfully, shaking all our hands warmly. "But what is happening?"

Takootu gazed sadly towards the jungle of Prickly-Pong and looked completely stunned when we explained what had happened. (We didn't tell him about finding Zeo's Treasure though. It just didn't seem the right time.)

We all felt extremely guilty because we could remember what Takootu had told us.

"You look after the island and the island will look after you."

We had failed to look after the island and now it was too late.

"I'm sorry," said Dad, sincerely. "It was me, I am the one to blame, I wouldn't listen to Jay or Sanjana about the Prickly-Pong. I was greedy. I'm not proud of myself or my actions."

We all apologized. It was all our faults. We were all to blame.

Takootu looked shocked and very, very sad. Then after a short spell of silence (which seemed like an hour) he spoke.

"We all is making the mistakes in life, but not so bad if we is learning from them. Yes?"

Takootu smiled and handed us a flask of water.

"Drink! You is looking thirsty."

The day was hot and the cold water refreshed us all. Takootu agreed to take us and the animals in his boat to a new island close by.

We had just finished moving the non-flying parrots and monkeys onto the 'Captain Cook', when Sanjana let out an almighty scream.

"What's the matter, Sanjana?" cried Dad, urgently.

"Out there!" Sanjana shrieked hysterically, looking out into the bay.

"It's Captain Red and his pirates! They've come back for Zeo's Treasure. They're going to kill us all!"

I gazed anxiously through my telescope... she was right! It was Captain Red and his pirates and we really were in trouble. We had no trees to hide in or monkeys to throw coconuts this time. We were all on our own!

Takootu looked alarmed and puzzled. "Why is they thinking you have Zeo's Treasure?"

"Because we have!" I cried, nervously. "We found a map and sailed to Muna Island. That's why we needed to build the boat. They're coming after us!"

Takootu looked at us with surprise and

suspicion. "You... is having... Zeo's treasure?!"

"Yes!" I replied. "It's hidden up there in the cave behind the waterfall! We want you to have it. It's for you and your people. It didn't seem right to mention it before."

Takootu looked at us all in total shock and disbelief.

"You is very full of the surprises, family Smith, but I like surprises. Especially I am liking this one!"

"The Black Pirates are coming too!" screamed Sanjana, looking terrified. "There are loads of them!"

Things weren't looking good for us or Zeo's treasure. One set of pirates was bad enough, but two sets of pirates was going to be a living nightmare...

"What are we going to do?!" wailed Sanjana, getting into a panic.

She wasn't the only one feeling frightened, but Takootu still seemed surprisingly calm.

"Do not worry, family Smith. It is being OK. Takootu will sort it out, you shall see."

Takootu pointed towards Giant Falls. "You all need to be hiding in cave with treasure. Quick! Hide! Go!"

But before we had time to get very far, Captain Red and his pirates were everywhere. On the beach, in the sea and by Takootu Falls, near the secret cave... we were surrounded!

"To the boat!" shouted Takootu, suddenly sounding alarmed and agitated. "Quick! Quick!"

Chapter 21

Trapped!

Things didn't look good. We had just managed to retreat back onto the boat in time, but Captain Red and his pirates had all our exits covered – we were trapped!

We stood out on deck, huddled together trembling with fear. I held Minoo close to my chest and prayed.

Captain Red strode rapidly towards us, looking angrier and more menacing than ever before. Some of the other pirates were there too and I recognised the first mate and the cabin-girl.

As they came closer, the Captain suddenly stopped and looked towards us quizzically. He seemed to recognise Takootu and what's more Takootu seemed to recognise him. They eyed each other up as though they were old enemies about to go into battle.

"Where is it?" demanded Captain Red, eyes bulging and raising his sword above his head in an extremely menacing manner.

"Where is what?" answered Takootu calmly, tapping a long black ebony staff lightly on the side of the boat.

"You know what!" replied Captain Red furiously. "Zeo's Treasure! The booty! Where be it?"

Takootu continued to tap his long ebony stick on the side of the boat, almost defiantly. I hadn't seen Takootu with a stick before and it looked like it was some sort of weapon.

"If I is knowing where it is, I am not telling the likes of you. It belongs to the people of Zeo!"

I couldn't believe it! Takootu was being so brave, standing there on his own in front of a gang of blood-thirsty buccaneers. I just hoped he knew what he was doing.

"You are being very bold, old man but it is futile," replied Captain Red moving closer to our boat. "We will feed you all to the sharks if you don't tell us, starting with the young girl!"

Suddenly from nowhere two of the meanest looking pirates appeared on deck and grabbed hold of Sanjana. She kicked and she screamed but they restrained her and held her still.

"Now I think you will tell us where it is?" sneered the Captain.

Captain Red waited for Takootu to reply, but he didn't get what he was expecting.

Takootu tapped his stick hard on the ground and then sprang towards Sanjana and the two pirates, twirling his staff above his head like a Samurai warrior going into battle!

I'm not sure quite what happened next because it happened so quickly, but within a matter of seconds Takootu had landed lightning-quick blows on both the pirates, who flew backwards into the sea with an almighty splash!

We all ran to Sanjana and comforted her. She was safe again, but for how long..? Captain Red was looking incensed.

"Scurvy-dogs! That was a very, very, VERY foolish thing to do!" he bellowed. "Now you will all die. You will drown at the bottom of the ocean or be eaten alive by the sharks. Prepare the plank, men!"

The pirates cheered and jeered and waved their swords and knives in the air, as the plank was brought forward close to the 'Captain Cook'.

"This is your last chance!" the Captain roared. "Tell us where the booty be hidden?"

The pirates cheered and jeered even louder.

Surely Takootu would have to tell them now…?

But Takootu didn't look as frightened as we were all feeling. He looked slowly up and down the beach and smiled.

"You is not the only ones who is looking for the treasure. Look behind you!"

* * *

Chapter 22

The Battle

Captain Red turned slowly and there storming up the beach were the Black Pirates! They looked lean and athletic and ready for battle.

"We're under attack!" bellowed Captain Red looking surprised but defiant. "Fight with valour, men! Like the pirates from the Golden Age. Fight for each other and die for each other!"

Captain Red and his men raced down the beach to face the Black Pirates for the second time that day and soon a vicious and violent battle was raging.

The Black Pirates wielded their long spears and sticks like experts in the martial arts. They moved like gymnasts, twisting and turning, jumping and dodging and then landing a decisive blow to the head or body. Battle cries filled the evening air...

"They're too strong for us, Captain!" cried one.

"And too quick!" yelled another.

Captain Red's men were no match for the Black Pirates. They looked slow and clumsy and their swords and long knives rarely landed a decisive blow on their more agile opponents.

Soon they were running for their lives, into the shallow waters, bewildered and beaten.

"Come back and fight like REAL Pirates!" barked Captain Red. "You feeble, weak, yellow-bellied excuse for a crew!"

The pirates continued to run for their lives into the deeper waters and soon they were swimming for the safety of their ship.

But Captain Red was made of sturdier

stuff – he wasn't finished. He looked up towards us angrily and let out a sinister laugh. "Follow me crew!"

He climbed up onto the 'Captain Cook', with his first mate, cabin-girl and two other crew closely behind him. As he moved slowly towards Takootu, he snarled menacingly.

"I know you have the treasure. It's here on this ship, isn't it? Give it to us now or you will live to regret it!"

Takootu gave it to them alright, but not what Captain Red was looking for! He twirled his ebony staff again like before, and within seconds three of the pirates had been dispatched into the sea with ease, including the first mate!

It was incredible! I couldn't believe it! Quiet, kind, friendly Takootu was a lethal, battle-hardened, Tahitian warrior!

Unfortunately for us, Captain Red was still standing and worse still he was pointing a hastily drawn pistol straight at Takootu!

"I'll blast you off this boat if you don't hand over the treasure!" barked the Captain, madly. "And that means all of you!"

Takootu froze. Surely he would have to give in now. There was no other choice...?

"That's not fair, Uncle!" shouted the cabin-girl, suddenly moving in front of Takootu. "You have always taught me to fight with valour and honour, like the pirates from the Golden Age."

"Yes, but sometimes needs must, my dear," replied the Captain, awkwardly.

"Pirates from the Golden Age would never shoot unarmed men, women or children!" continued the cabin-girl, forcefully.

"I'll fight anyhow I do please, so long as I gets my hands on that booty!" replied the Captain, angrily. "So get out of my way, little girl! This is men's work!"

"Don't you talk to me like that!" shouted the cabin-girl, rebelliously, waving her sword in his face.

I couldn't believe it. The cabin-girl was daring to challenge the word of Captain Red, and what's more - HE was her uncle!

Takootu took his chance. While the Captain was distracted, he twirled his ebony stick one more time and seconds later the Captain's pistol was flying into the Pacific Ocean!

"Scurvy dogs!" ranted the Captain furiously."Now look what you've done, girl. I knew it was a mistake to bring you!"

"Better this way, Uncle," replied Kat the cabin-girl, suddenly launching a fierce attack on Takootu. "We can take him using skill and steel not powder and guns!"

Soon the cabin-girl, Captain Red and Takootu were all locked into an epic combat. The cabin-girl fought as ferociously as the Captain and she certainly knew how to use a sword. Takootu was having to use all his skills to defend himself. I just wished I could be doing something to help...

It looked like the fight would never end, then all of a sudden the Captain landed an almighty blow and Takootu's black ebony staff shattered in two!

We all gasped! Takootu was unarmed! His weapon lay in pieces on the deck, not far from where we were huddled. We had to do something but what...?

"Now I think you will tell us!" came the triumphant sneer of the Captain, his blade pointing menacingly at Takootu's heart.

Suddenly I had an idea! I grabbed

hold of my telescope (which was hanging around my neck as always) and threw it to Takootu – calling his name as I did.

Thankfully, it was a good throw and Takootu caught it in mid-air, just in time to deflect the blood-thirsty thrust of Captain Red!

The Captain cursed again and cast a venomous look in my direction. Then he launched another ferocious attack on Takootu who had somehow managed to pick up his broken staff.

"Leave him to me, cabin-girl. I want to finish him myself!"

Takootu continued to battle on, bravely defending himself with Grandad's telescope in one hand and his broken staff in the other. But things didn't look good. He couldn't hold out for much longer...

"You'd better make it quick, Uncle!" cried the cabin-girl urgently, "The Black Pirates are approaching - they'll be here any second!"

The cabin-girl was right. The Black Pirates were speeding towards us and were just a few metres away...

"Scurvy-dogs!" cursed the Captain madly, glancing an eye in our direction. "Maybe we need to take a hostage or two!"

His staff might have been broken, but Takootu's spirit certainly wasn't. Just at that moment, Takootu landed a series of powerful blows which sent a dazed and defeated Captain overboard and into the Pacific Ocean! The cabin-girl looked beaten too and dived in after him.

"This isn't the end," spluttered Captain Red defiantly, surfacing from the depths, with slimy seaweed tangled into his beard. "I shall return!"

A huge sense of elation and relief came over us, but the feeling didn't last long.

As Captain Red swam for his life to escape the sharks, we were left to face our new enemy - the terrifying Black Pirates!

No one could save us now, not even Takootu. We would have to hand over the treasure to them. It didn't seem fair on Takootu after all he had done to help us, but there was no way out this time...

* * *

Chapter 23

The Surprise

The wave of Black Pirates moved stealthily across the sand, their threatening gaze fixed firmly upon us.

"You is not worrying, family Smith," said Takootu calmly. "Everything is being OK."

But none of us could believe Takootu's brave words. We huddled together on the boat, anxiously waiting and wondering. What was going to happen to us? Would they feed us to the sharks? Bury us alive? Or worse, boil us in a pot of hot sea water and then eat us for supper? This could be it! No more playing coconut catch with Minoo! No more parties at Grandma's and Grandad's...?

They were getting quite close now and we could see their heavily tattooed faces, frowning at us fiercely. They looked like warriors from the past – strong and determined.

We were expecting the worst, when all of a sudden something extraordinary happened! Just as they got within touching distance of the 'Captain Cook', the Black Pirates fell to their knees and started chanting...

The chanting was loud and repetitive, in some strange language we didn't understand. Was this part of some ancient ritual? Were they offering us up to their Gods before they cooked us alive...?

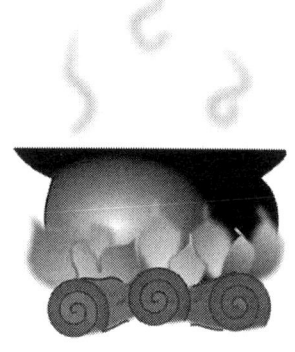

All of a sudden, Takootu stood up from his seat and raised his broken ebony staff above his head. To our astonishment, the chanting stopped instantly and the Black Pirates looked up towards Takootu as though he was a long-lost friend!

Then Takootu started to speak to the Black Pirates in a strange language we didn't understand. They hung on his every word, like Year 2 listening to Mr Evans (our deputy head), in school assembly.

Suddenly, the Black Pirates sprang to their feet excitedly and started jumping onto the boat.

"You is not worrying, family Smith!" shouted Takootu, beaming from ear to ear. "They is my friends! They is your friends!"

Within seconds, the Black Pirates were swarming all around us on board the 'Captain Cook'. But to our surprise and utter relief they weren't attacking us or feeding us to the sharks, quite the opposite! They were smiling and patting us on our backs cheerfully.

They were our...

FRIENDS!

Takootu told us that the Black Pirates weren't pirates at all. They were his family tribe called the Radi and what's more, he was their CHIEF! Chief Takootu! They all believed in the God Zeo and had spent their lives trying to find the lost treasure and return it to sacred Radimatu.

"You is all heroes!" shouted Chief Takootu. "We have been searching for Zeo's Treasure for years and years and now you is finding it. We is all so, so happy!"

"Let's show them where it is, Chief!" I cried excitedly to Takootu, as I leapt off the boat into the shallow water. I dashed up the beach towards Takootu

Falls. "Follow me!" I cried. "If you want to find Zeo's Treasure!"

Soon the twenty or so Radi warriors were speeding up the beach close behind, with Chief Takootu and Sanjana alongside me.

Takootu and Sanjana helped me bring the treasure chest out from its special hiding place and we set it down on the beach carefully.

The Radi warriors looked on eagerly in awe and anticipation.

"You open it!" I cried excitedly to Takootu. "It's your treasure!"

Takootu looked almost in tears, as he carefully eased the heavy wooden lid ajar, with his broken ebony stick. The buzz of excitement from the Radi tribe suddenly fell silent.

We all watched as Takootu looked carefully over the treasure. Suddenly he started to rummage more urgently, as though he was looking for something in particular.

A few seconds later he pulled out an object that looked like a gold pendant and held it up above his head to his tribe. Then excitedly, he seized the gold pendant that was hanging around his neck and held it up next to it, for all the Radi to see. They looked exactly the same!

The Radi gasped! It was the treasure they were looking for. Zeo's Treasure, that had been stolen from them hundreds of years ago and the special gold pendant proved it was genuine. It was the Lost Treasure of Zeo!

Takootu wiped a tear from his eye and then as the whole contents of the chest became visible, a huge cry of delight went up from the Radi.

Within moments, they were leaping high into the air with elation and hugging each other and all of us. They cheered and they chanted and danced around the treasure. It was as though their national team had just scored the winning goal in the World Cup Final!

The chanting and dancing went on for quite a while. Then the Radi took it in turns to take a good look at the priceless jewels. Each time they did, they knelt down by the side of the sacred chest and said a prayer to Zeo.

"This is great day!" declared Takootu excitedly, watching the treasure being carefully loaded onto the 'Captain Cook'. "Later we is returning the treasure to Radimatu and all people will be amazed and so happy. We is having another party I am thinking!"

* * *

Chapter 24

Second Chance

Amid all the fun and celebration we had almost forgotten about the monkeys and birds left on Takootu's boat and what had become of our beautiful island. We gazed sadly at the mass of giant Prickly-Pong engulfing the tall palms and our hearts sank once more.

We ran back to the 'Captain Cook' and checked on the monkeys and parrots. They still looked very poorly and Minoo was quieter than I had ever seen him, even after all the recent celebration. There was still no chattering or mischief-making. It wasn't the Minoo we all knew, but at least he was alive.

"We is going to new island now," cried Takootu cheerfully. "New home for monkeys and parrots and you! It is being closer to Radimatu, home of Radi. We will visit you often. All of us. You is being our family now!"

The Radi tribe smiled and waved from their canoes. We were to be given a guided escort to our new island!

Suddenly I felt a lot more positive about things. We were being given another chance, a new start. As the boat moved out to sea, I looked back with Minoo in my arms.

"We won't make the same mistake twice," I whispered. "I promise."

I noticed that Sanjana and Mum were both crying and I felt like crying too. Saying goodbye to something or someone you love isn't easy and we had loved our stay on Gigantuki Island.

* * *

* * *

Chapter 25

Island Zeo

It didn't take us long to reach our new island. Sanjana suggested we called it 'Zeo', as it was the god of 'new life' as well as war. Takootu was very pleased with our choice and so were the Radi, who performed a celebration dance as we walked ashore for the first time.

Island Zeo looked very similar to Gigantuki Island before the 'you know what' got out of hand. There were green and red parrots, SMALL Prickly-Pong and trees – beautiful, green palm trees!

We all thought we were extremely lucky to get a second chance on a new island and we were determined not to make the same mistake twice.

Minoo and the other animals settled in well and soon they were back to full health. There were no monkeys living on Zeo when we arrived, but before long it was just like old times. Minoo and his monkey friends playing coconut catch and hide-and-seek in the trees, with me of course!

Everyone seemed to be getting on better too. Sanjana played with Minoo and me all the time, and Mum and Dad even joined in the odd game of coconut cricket.

Takootu and the Radi visited us often and we had beach barbecues almost every Saturday, which were fantastic fun! They taught us how to catch the local fish, canoe around the island and how to defend ourselves with the long sticks, which they called Rodu.

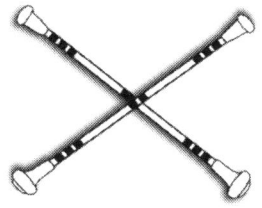

Takootu would often pretend to be Captain Red and we would always try to take him down using our newly-taught fighting skills. Sadly, he was always too quick for us and we always ended up on our backs, pleading for mercy!

Thankfully we never ran in to the 'real' Captain Red again, so we never had to try out our fighting skills for proper!

* * *

All good things sadly come to an end, and after many fantastic weeks on

Island Zeo, our holiday was over and it was time to go back home to England. I didn't want to go, none of us did, but we knew we had to.

I was desperate to take Minoo with us. I would miss him so much and I knew he would miss me, but I also knew I could never take him home. It wouldn't be fair for him, stuck in a cold dark house all day was no life for a lively, playful, mischievous monkey.

Suddenly I heard Minoo's call and I looked up in the tree and there he was swinging from branch to branch and making silly noises with his monkey friends. He looked so happy. I just had to accept it – I would never see Minoo again after tomorrow. All I would have was our memories, but what wonderful memories they would be!

Takootu arrived early the next morning to collect us. It was the one time I wasn't pleased to see the 'Captain Cook'. Takootu had brought a few of the Radi with him to help us load on our bags.

Minoo could sense something was wrong. He wasn't his usual chattery self. He hadn't eaten breakfast with me like he always did, and had taken himself up his favourite tree. He was now sitting very quietly, looking out to sea.

Takootu could tell I was upset too and tried to make a few silly jokes about Captain Red to cheer me up, but they didn't work. I was feeling too sad. What's more, I knew I was going to be feeling like it for a very long time.

When all our bags were safely packed onto the 'Captain Cook', Takootu stood up on deck with a glint in his eye and told us he had some special news.

"First I is giving you both a gift, to help you remember us every day!"

Takootu proudly handed Sanjana what looked like a brand new Rodu and then he gave one to me too!

"Rodu is hand-made from tree on sacred Radimatu. You must practise every day until you is very good - like my Radi warriors!"

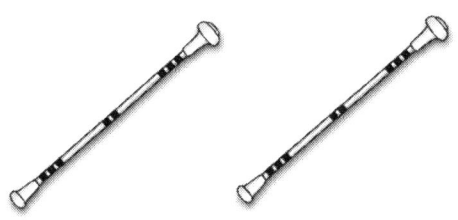

This really was a special present for us both. The Radi clapped and cheered. We would miss them too, but not as much as we would miss Takootu and Minoo.

Takootu continued speaking. "I is not finished yet family Smith. Takootu is having a second thing to say to you..." Takootu paused and suddenly looked quite serious.

"Takootu is not saying the goodbye to you, family Smith," he declared with a beaming smile across his face. "You must be coming back next year to celebrate grand opening of museum!"

Takootu bowed respectfully, like we were royalty and presented Mum and Dad with a handwritten letter.

"You all is famous!" he continued. "You is ones who is discovering 'Lost Treasure of Zeo'. It is being on display at Radimatu Museum for very first time, next July. It is all there in letter!"

I was stunned. I couldn't believe it! A chance to see Minoo and Takootu again! Surely, it was too good to be true?

"Can we?" I asked Mum and Dad, not daring to hear the answer 'No'. "Can we please, please, PLEASE?"

"Pretty please?" cried Sanjana. "We'll be ever so good all year!"

"I'll promise to work hard at school and keep my bedroom tidy!" I begged, kneeling at their feet.

Mum and Dad looked at the letter, then at each other and then looked back at us and smiled.

"We'll take that as a yes!" I squealed, jumping in the air with delight. I'd never felt so happy. I just ran around hugging everyone in sight! Sanjana was doing the same and even Takootu, who usually only shook hands, joined in our celebration and gave us all big hugs too!

Then I shouted up to Minoo in the tree excitedly, "Minoo! Minoo!"

He ignored me at first, as though he hadn't heard me, but I kept on calling him. "Minoo! Minoo! We are coming back! We are coming back!"

Suddenly Minoo swung round and started chattering and pulling funny faces like he always did. Then he dived off his branch into the air and completed an amazing mid-air somersault! Seconds later, Minoo was skillfully swinging down from high up in the tree and before I knew it, he had landed on my head!

I wrestled him off affectionately, threw him high into the air and then caught him in my arms! Just like I always did when he was being mischievous. (which was most of the time!) It was so amazing to think I would see Minoo again! I gave him one last hug and then he scampered back up his favourite tree to see us off.

So that was that. We said our last goodbyes to the Radi and set off in the 'Captain Cook' with Takootu for home.

Chapter 26

Lessons Learned

Grandma and Grandad gave us a wonderful welcome home. Grandad had made a brilliant blue banner for the front of the house, with balloons everywhere! Grandma had made the biggest chocolate cake I'd ever seen and there was even more food than usual. It was all so yummy and the flapjack tasted better than ever.

"I've missed this, Grandma!" I said, munching happily on my sixth piece. "And you of course!".

"And we've missed you!" replied Grandma, giving us all more hugs and kisses.

They wanted to know all about our year away and they couldn't believe what we had to tell them. Especially about Captain Red and the treasure. They thought we were making up stories at first!

"Real pirates?" exclaimed Grandma, looking scared.

"What an adventure!", cried Grandad, excitedly, pretending to sword fight me with his walking stick. "I wish I'd been there with you! ARGHH!"

Grandad let out a blood-curdling cry and collapsed on the sofa playing dead. Grandma smiled and then raised her eyebrows in the way she always did and it suddenly felt very good to be home.

But not everything had gone well on our trip and after tea we told them all about the giant Prickly-Pong and how it had destroyed our beautiful island.

"How heartbreaking for you all," said

Grandma, looking upset. "Those lovely trees and those poor animals, how terrible!"

"That's the problem," cried Grandad, passionately, as he got up off the sofa. "Everything is so connected, so finely balanced, we don't realise how careful we need to be until it's too late!"

"Learning from one's mistakes – that's the important thing," said Grandma cheerfully.

"That's what Takootu said!" I cried excitedly.

We certainly had learnt from our mistakes and it was something we never ever wanted to experience again. We needed to be more careful in the future, we knew that now.

"Tell us some more about Captain Red and Chief Takootu!" demanded Grandad eagerly. "I want some more adventure!"

Grandad got his wish and we spent the rest of the evening telling them all about the fierce Captain and his not so fierce crew. He particularly enjoyed hearing about the encounter where his telescope had saved Takootu's life and ours!

"I told you it would come in handy!" cried Grandad, proudly examining the scratches and dents on the side of his telescope.

"Sorry about the damage, Grandad."

"Don't be!" replied Grandad excitedly. "Scars of battle! I wish I'd been there to see it!"

Although we had regrets, we certainly had lots of happy memories from our trip together. Memories that we would never ever forget. The most special part of our adventure for me was making new friends, especially with Takootu and of course Minoo.

Since coming home, everything feels a

little bit different than before. Me and Sanjana are playing together a little more and arguing a little less. I'm even starting to enjoy school some days, especially when the homework is to write about your favourite holiday, like it is this week!

I used my holiday diary. The one mum made us do every morning on the island. I'm glad she did now. Mind you, I could never have written it all on my own - Sanjana has helped me loads. Maybe having a 'super-smart' twin sister isn't so bad after all?!

Our holiday had turned out to be the most exciting adventure of my life so far, but I hope there are many more adventures to come. Starting next summer when we open the Museum of Radimatu. I can't wait to meet up with Minoo and Takootu again!

* * *

So that's about it for now...

I told you I left a chest full of treasure worth thousands of pounds on a desert island.

So... do you think I was completely crazy or would you have done the same in my situation?

The End

Dear Reader

I hope you enjoyed this book? If you did, you may be interested in reading the next adventure in the series which will be out next year!

Prickly-Pong Island
&
Captain Red's Revenge

Grandma's Flapjack

'Crunch'

1) First, lightly smear a baking tray (25 cm x 35 cm) with a little butter (or lard), and line with a generous sheet of baking parchment or greaseproof paper. (Press the paper firmly onto the baking tray and into the corners.)

2) Next, weigh out 9 oz (250g) of rolled oats and place in large bowl.

3) Then, weigh out 3 oz (85g) of sugar and add to the oats.

4) After that, weigh out 6 oz (170g) of butter and place in small saucepan.

5) Add 3 loaded dessert spoons of golden syrup to the butter. (In hot weather it is difficult to judge and very sticky!)

6) Place saucepan on a low setting to melt butter and carefully raise the heat until the contents melt and the mixture froths.

7) Pour frothing mixture onto oats and sugar and mix in well.

8) Carefully spoon the mixture onto the lined tray and smooth mixture up to edges carefully with a clean metal spoon.

9) Finally, place in middle of oven at gas mark 4 (Electric 180 C). (*I suggest laying a large piece of foil loosely over the flapjack to prevent burning.

The delicious 'Crunch' should be ready in 15 to 20 minutes.

Cut into squares (big or small!) and ...
ENJOY!

Books by Christopher Davies

If you would like to find out about, or purchase other books written by the author, please check out the Author's Page for Christopher Davies on Amazon.co.uk

89526699R00124

Made in the USA
Columbia, SC
22 February 2018